JOHNNY TOWNSEND
MURDER AT THE
JACK OFF CLUB

Murder at the Jack Off Club

When a miserable S.O.B. is murdered at the J.O.B. (Jack Off Buddies) party on Seattle's Capitol Hill, detectives find sixty naked suspects. Bruce Chealander, unfortunately, is suspect #1 after his public argument with the victim just an hour earlier. That's unfortunate for Detective Demir Altan, too, as he finds himself drawn to the potential murderer. But Bruce isn't the only suspect. Salvador Castro had three exes at the sex club, and several of the volunteers hated the guy as well.

But when a second man is killed at another jack off party two weeks later, and this victim only has ties to Bruce, he's back as Suspect #1.

Is someone trying to deflect suspicion from the first murder by murdering someone else? Is there a gay serial killer on the loose?

None of this is helping improve Bruce's strained marriage with his Duwamish partner.

Bruce does *not* want to get involved in the investigation, but with increasing political tensions in addition to the sexual tension at home, he can't let this one bit of gay culture—and freedom—slip away without a fight.

Will his blundering efforts help find the killer or spur the man to act again?

And can Bruce stay out of jail long enough to discover the real killer before he or any more of his friends end up dead?

Praise for Johnny Townsend

"Townsend's prose [in *Murder at the Jack Off Club*] is punchy and evocative, and his depictions of the characters' relationships and heartaches are frank and nuanced….a sometimes cheesy but ultimately affecting saga of love and death….a rich portrait of gay life."

Kirkus Reviews

In *Zombies for Jesus*, "Townsend isn't writing satire, but deeply emotional and revealing portraits of people who are, with a few exceptions, quite lovable."

Kel Munger, *Sacramento News and Review*

In *Sex among the Saints,* "Townsend writes with a deadpan wit and a supple, realistic prose that's full of psychological empathy….he takes his protagonists' moral struggles seriously and invests them with real emotional resonance."

Kirkus Reviews

Gayrabian Nights is "an allegorical tour de force…a hard-core emotional punch."

Gay. Guy. Reading and Friends

Inferno in the French Quarter: The UpStairs Lounge Fire is "a gripping account of all the horrors that transpired that night, as well as a respectful remembrance of the victims."

Terry Firma, Patheos

"Johnny Townsend's 'Partying with St. Roch' [in the anthology *Latter-Gay Saints*] tells a beautiful, haunting tale."

Kent Brintnall, Out in Print: Queer Book Reviews

The Washing of Brains has "A lovely writing style, and each story [is] full of unique, engaging characters....immensely entertaining."

Rainbow Awards

In *Dead Mankind Walking*, "Townsend writes in an energetic prose that balances crankiness and humor....A rambunctious volume of short, well-crafted essays..."

Kirkus Reviews

Murder at the Jack Off Club

Johnny Townsend

Print ISBN: 978-1-961525-28-3
Ebook ISBN: 978-1-961525-29-0

Printed on acid-free paper.

2025

First Edition

Cover design by GalsCreations

Contents

Chapter One………………………………………………..9
Chapter Two……………………………………………...26
Chapter Three…………………………………………….44
Chapter Four……………………………………………...50
Chapter Five………………………………………………59
Chapter Six………………………………………………..69
Chapter Seven…………………………………………...79
Chapter Eight……………………………………...……...89
Chapter Nine……………………………………………..101
Chapter Ten………………………………………………110
Chapter Eleven…………………………………………..118
Chapter Twelve…………………………………………..130
Chapter Thirteen………………………………………….138
Chapter Fourteen…………………………………………149
Chapter Fifteen…………………………………………...159
Chapter Sixteen…………………………………………..169
Chapter Seventeen……………………………………….177
Chapter Eighteen…………………………………………189
Chapter Nineteen………………………………………...199
Chapter Twenty…………………………………………..214
Epilogue…………………………………………………...219
Books by Johnny Townsend………………………224
What Readers Have Said…………………………236

Chapter One

"No!" Salvador thrust a well-manicured finger in my face. "I told you the linens *cannot* touch the floor!"

I gritted my teeth. "I can't adjust them until I see if they touch or not," I countered, struggling to keep my tone neutral. This was the fourth time tonight the volunteer coordinator had singled me out in front of everyone.

"It's not rocket science," Salvador said.

"I didn't think it was." I was tempted to spout an equation for acceleration I remembered from my college days, but it had been four decades since those days and I didn't want to flub it.

Or engage with Salvador any longer than necessary.

"Well, *fix it*, Bruce!"

Tonight was my fifth time volunteering with set-up for Seattle's bi-monthly Jack Off Buddies event. *"Come to JOB for a hand job!"* The group met on the ground floor and basement of a hundred-and-ten-year-old building in the Pike/Pine corridor on Capitol Hill, barely a gay neighborhood anymore. I'd lived in Seattle for years and still needed a pneumonic device to remember which street came first. Pine was the more northern of the two. N for north. Pike was the more southern. K for KKK.

My father had done his Mormon missionary service in Alabama. I remembered the stories.

I adjusted the linen on the padded bench so it no longer touched the floor. Linens had to fully cover the back and surface of each piece of furniture in the playroom, given that hordes of naked men were about to descend on the place. If the linen dragged even an inch on the floor, someone would step on it, the movement would pull the linen off the furniture, and we'd soon have sanitation issues.

I knew all this, of course. Salvador repeated it a dozen times during every event while we set up.

"Will this one work better?" Chris pulled another beige linen out of a blue plastic bag. He held it up to gauge its size.

"Let's give it a shot." I nodded my thanks. Chris had volunteered in the past, but I'd never met him before. He was about forty, a good twenty years my junior, slim, and blond. Well, blond*ish*, if you didn't count the roots. His face still bore tiny acne scars from his youth, not nearly as far in his past as in mine. He wore tight jeans and an even tighter T-shirt that read, "What's your gaydar telling you?", carrying himself as if he understood he was good looking, which he was, but without the usual arrogance that accompanied such knowledge.

The cloth rabbit patches affixed to his shoes probably influenced my assessment. I hoped they hinted he liked to fuck in addition to giving hand jobs.

Chris and I folded the new piece of linen in two so it would fit without dragging and were soon able to move on to the next piece of furniture, a large, padded cube more than three feet high. I pulled out a heavy, thick linen from one of the plastic bags.

"No, no, no!" Salvador shouted from across the room. "That one won't fit! Pick another one!"

Chris looked at me, trying to hide his grin.

"Can I at least look at the linen and evaluate it before deciding where to put it?" I called back across the room.

"No! Just do what I tell you! Good god, this isn't rocket science!"

Chris reached into the bag and pulled out another linen. It was slightly too small. Before Salvador could say anything—thankfully, he was preoccupied now with bitching at Stu, another volunteer—I pulled yet another linen from a different bag.

"There'd better be some nice dick here tonight," Chris whispered with another grin.

I held up the new linen to see if it might work. "Are you a green wrist bander or a red wrist bander?" I asked as casually as I could.

He chuckled. "I usually wear the green ones, but not on nights when I volunteer."

I cocked my head. "Yeah?"

"I don't want to give *that* guy permission to touch me without asking." Chris helped me adjust the new linen, which we finally managed to position correctly over the padded cube. "But *you* don't have to ask later," he added. "I'll give you permission now."

I smiled.

I'd been married almost twenty-five years, but Tommy and I rarely had sex these days. As I grew older, as climate change grew worse, and as the political climate grew more precarious, I'd decided several months ago to make the most of whatever time and health I had left. A Jack Off Buddies party offered a reasonably safe space for sex. No oral. No anal. No fingering. And no docking (I had to look that one up). Only jacking and kissing.

Which reminded me. I'd never helped set up the two restrooms on previous occasions, but I wanted to do that tonight. I'd be out of Salvador's sight. And I was sick of linens. The other volunteers could finish covering the chairs and sofas. The laundry service JOB used sent back a different batch of linens every time. I never worked with the same linens twice. Finding pieces the right size was maddening, even without being bitched at.

"I'll make sure there's mouthwash in the restrooms," I said. "And I'll swish thoroughly before the doors open at 7:00. In case you like to kiss."

Chris smiled. "I do."

I left Chris and Ofer, an Israeli immigrant who'd recently moved to the U.S. to escape growing fascism back home, to finish covering the remaining furniture. Marin, a giant, heavyset black man in his thirties, almost leaped across the room to help, glancing back over his shoulder as if making sure Salvador wasn't coming for him. The volunteer coordinator had bitched at him earlier for putting the wrong chairs in the reception area. "The ones with the gold legs go out front! Not those! Good grief! This isn't rocket science!"

I opened the storage bin containing the bathroom supplies and grabbed some mouthwash.

The next forty-five minutes were much the same. Salvador bitched at me for not putting *full* containers of mouthwash in the bathrooms. "We don't want to run out in the middle of an event!" he shouted. "If a bottle's not full, fill it from another bottle."

Okay. That made sense. But why not simply *explain* it?

I didn't set up the chairs in the basement correctly for New Member Orientation, another task I'd chosen for the first time to avoid the man. I didn't set up the tub of padlocks the right way.

Back upstairs, I took some photos of the playroom before any participants arrived, hoping to convince Tommy to join me another evening. "You can't take pictures of people without their permission!" Salvador hissed.

"I don't think anyone's sitting in the bowl of wrist bands." I put my phone away. "Unless you can see fairies no one else can."

I wasn't Salvador's only target, of course. He bitched at Marin for putting a chair too close to the wall, where it might damage the paint or some of the erotic artwork hanging throughout the room. He bitched at Stu for positioning the "Lockers this way" sign on the wrong post. He bitched at Chris for putting one too many small trash bins next to a table.

"Get rid of that trash can!" Salvador demanded from the far side of the room.

Chris looked about for a place to set it down.

"I said toss it!"

Chris flung the trash can fifteen feet across the floor toward the storage closet. He smiled sweetly, but no one did a thing like that unless they were peeved. I sent a supportive wink in his direction, but his eyes were fixed on Salvador.

I'd already decided this would be my last time volunteering for set up. It was early December, and before leaving the house I'd looked up next year's schedule on the JOB website and discovered that Salvador was scheduled for every single set-up session for the upcoming year. The break-down/clean-up session was too inconvenient after evening events since I wouldn't get home on public transit until after 11:00. But I could volunteer to clean up after the Saturday afternoon events. I'd already signed up to help with one in January, one in February, and one in March.

It was almost playtime, I kept reminding myself. My libido was quickly evaporating, but once the doors opened and men emerged from the locker room in the basement wearing nothing but wrist bands, perhaps I could revive it. Just get the damn set up done, Bruce, I told myself.

But I apparently took too long to fill the water bottles in the kitchen. Salvador barged in and ordered me to use the better faucet. The one blocked by several large pieces of kitchen equipment which I had no intention of moving. "You're slowing everyone down!" He took a deep breath. "And I need to talk to you about your placement of the hand sanitizer in the bathrooms!"

"I'll bet you do."

Salvador stopped, motionless for perhaps the first time this evening. He was fortyish, a bit heavy, with a deep diagonal crease on the left side of his forehead and an unpleasant mole just above and to the right of his mouth. It was his personality, though, that made him unattractive. "What did you say?"

"I'm not psychic. You could always write the instructions down and put them in a binder every volunteer could refer to. Or email them as a PDF so we could review everything before coming in for our shifts."

Salvador huffed. "You can't remember simple instructions?" His lip curled. "It's not rocket science."

I handed him a filled water bottle and loose screw top. "I'll head back to the restrooms," I said, brushing past him.

In the hallway, Marin's eyes widened. He must have overheard.

Just get through this evening, I kept telling myself. We were almost done.

But we weren't done *yet*. Salvador was unhappy with how Chris and I set up the end tables throughout the play area. Paper towels, a package of wipes, a bowl of tiny lube cups, and a small battery-operated lamp went on each table. But we hadn't set it all up the *right way*. We had to press the On button *seven* times to get the lights the correct color.

"Chris!" Salvador ordered. "Bruce!" He pointed at a painting of a giant blue penis. "Face the wall! Now!"

What the hell?

I wondered if I'd forgotten to post a sign on the wall. We turned as directed. I wouldn't let him think I was rattled.

"Quiz!" Salvador said. "What goes on the end tables?" He paused half a second. "Answer me! What goes on the end tables?"

"Um, paper towels," Chris began.

But I turned around. "You've got to be fucking kidding me," I said. "Are we in a Victorian boarding school? Get a goddamn grip on yourself."

Salvador's face darkened, his eyes seeming to narrow and widen at the same time, like the lens focused on the stairwell scene in *Vertigo*. "Go downstairs and set up the chairs in the locker room!"

"Will you be coming down, too?"

"Go!" he growled. "And put the right linens on every chair! I'll be checking on you!"

I grabbed a few linens from the storage closet, where I found Stu hiding beside the one chair we kept on the ground floor for disabled men who couldn't navigate the stairs to undress in the official locker room. He was trembling, but I wasn't sure if he was scared of Salvador or of me. After all, I'd been pretty loud, too.

"Is this a jack off club," I asked, "or an S&M club?" I forced a smile. "This public humiliation crap isn't working for me."

"I know where we could get a ball gag," Stu whispered. He was in his upper sixties, a few years older than me, with thinning white hair, thin and wispy himself, rather like the figure in Munch's "The Scream."

"Oh, I think any old pair of underwear will do."

Stu giggled.

The last task before opening was to refill the storage bin with tiny cups of lube. I usually enjoyed this part most, just sitting and chatting with the other volunteers gathered around the large, padded cube as we worked. Tonight, I stayed in the restroom, making sure the cups were in the right place and the soap dispensers filled.

I gargled three times with mouthwash in the hopes that Chris had been serious about kissing.

The harsh light in the restroom did little for my confidence, but most of the guys who came to JOB were welcoming of a variety of ages and body types. Not everyone. But most. Knowing this, of course, didn't magically erase all my self-doubts.

I had wrinkles but not too many. I still had most of my hair. No double chin but some looseness in the skin on my neck. Clean shaven. Eyebrows I kept trimmed when I trimmed my nose hairs. Dark blue-framed glasses which I kept on during the festivities even though they seemed to turn some guys off.

Looking any lower at my reflection was a bit like doomscrolling online. I knew ahead of time it would be bad but couldn't stop myself.

Unimpressive nipples and chest hair. Less impressive stomach. An it-is-what-it-is dick. And then some halfway decent legs.

I could be a model if I wore green screen over everything but my legs.

I'd never been a 9, even in my prime, so I didn't have a lot of looks to lose. It was easier to fade from a 6.5 to a 5.9 than from a 9 to a 6.5, a well-worn rock to begin with now just slightly more worn. As long as I could look at myself in the mirror and continue to see someone "above average," even if I was only slightly over the 50% mark, it was the most I could hope for.

I still found my husband Tommy attractive and wished the feeling was mutual.

I wished he'd at least let me watch him beat off.

I wished he'd bring someone home to play with, even if I couldn't take part. He needed something I couldn't give him, and I wished he could have it.

I'd try harder to get Tommy to come to JOB next time.

A man who wasn't a volunteer popped into the bathroom, naked. Time to head downstairs and grab a locker before they were all taken. Volunteers got in free. Others paid $20. On my way down, I passed Chris on his way up. He reached over and tweaked my nipple through my shirt. Hopefully, the evening was going to turn out okay.

Other than my glasses and a green band on each wrist, the only other items I wore tonight were shoes and socks. Some men walked around barefoot, but while I wasn't averse to licking cum off a cute guy's foot, that was prohibited activity here, so there was no reason not to avoid athlete's foot while we were avoiding most other communicable infections. I put my wristwatch in my jeans pocket before shutting the locker, took off my Do Not Resuscitate necklace—not a sexy piece of jewelry, in case you were wondering—and even removed my fidget wedding ring, the only kind of ring I could wear without chafing my skin.

Silver with a blue chain I could spin around and around my ring finger.

But sometimes at JOB, you could be working a different dick with each hand, and ringless hand jobs were decidedly more satisfying for all parties.

The lights had dimmed by the time the doors opened, so it was difficult to see the artwork now. Nude paintings of men, nude paintings of women, paintings of male or female genitalia. A wall sculpture featuring a purple vulva. Most of the work was amateurish but still fun.

Even my husband's works were better than some of these. Perhaps if I could get Tommy to submit something to the gallery, I could then get him to come and participate at an event.

I preferred works by Nicolae Negura or Astra Zero over the kind of pieces hanging here, perhaps a watercolor by Brenden Sanborn or oils by Igor Sychev. The oils were way out of my price range, of course, though I did own a few prints by Anthony Hurd, celebrating gay cowboys.

I liked my art to show two or three men together so it was clear I wasn't only looking at a beautiful man but at a gay couple or throuple.

Neither Tommy nor I had the energy for another full partner in our relationship, but sometimes, I wished I'd tried for a triad when I was younger.

At least twenty men were already sitting on the fresh linens all about the playroom. One man lay face down on a massage table, but no one had approached him yet. Most of the sitting men stole glances at each other, hoping someone else would make the first move. Almost everyone, except the man with his face in the massage table face hole, looked up at the screen where short videos of men masturbating played on a loop.

A Latino up on the screen shot onto his chest. A black man's cum hit his chin as he scrambled to catch a drop with his tongue. An Asian man scrunched his face in ecstatic agony as he burst onto his T-shirt. A white guy casually stroked until a flood of white spread out over his pubes. He barely even blinked when he came.

The videos gave everyone something to do until the real action started. The best event I'd attended so far had been the semi-annual Countdown party, where everyone was asked to edge until 8:00, when we were all encouraged to ejaculate at the same time.

If you've never been in a room with sixty naked men cumming simultaneously, it's quite the sight to behold.

Of course, there were plenty of gay men who were appalled at clubs like this, friends who looked down on me for participating. "You're *married!*" they'd remind me.

"We've been open since the day we met," I'd remind them. Even members of marginalized sex minorities could hold exceptionally Puritan views at times. The sex positive rules at JOB were the main reason I came here instead of going to the baths. Sex should be celebrated, I felt, and never used as a weapon, either physically or psychologically, and what constituted a safe space in some other places wasn't enough for me.

I remembered overhearing my zone leader in Rome telling another missionary, "Can you imagine Anziano Chealander on his wedding night?"

Shaming people was a sin and gay men were as good at it as anyone else.

"We treat everyone with respect," the JOB rules insisted, "whether we're interested in playing or not."

Too bad that rule didn't seem to apply to volunteers.

I found a spot near a four-foot-high speaker acting as an end table and watched a ginger with a dad bod welcome a heavyset, dark haired bear a few years younger. The guy with the dad bod was an otter on his way to becoming a bear himself, but still quite striking, both by traditional standards and bear standards.

A deaf white guy in his twenties on the sofa just beyond them wrote something on a notepad and showed it to an Asian man around fifty sitting next to him. The Asian man nodded and they began fondling each other.

I'd taken two dick pills before leaving home. Just one didn't get the job done. But sometimes, simply watching without participating was all I needed to have a good time. Seeing other people enjoy themselves, connect in a truly intimate way, even if only briefly, made me smile. I found it beautiful.

I felt a hand on my arm and turned.

"Hey, troublemaker." It was Chris.

"You're the one who threw the chair."

He chuckled and reached for my dick. His hand was already pre-lubed. I quickly grabbed a small cup of lube from a nearby table and started stroking him, too. It was a bit early to jack off, barely 7:20. Doors wouldn't even close until 8:00.

Some of the younger men could probably beat off twice but I'd rarely been able to do such a thing even in my youth.

"Mmmh," I moaned. "You do that well."

"I do other things well, too." He leaned over and nuzzled my ear. Then he kissed my jaw. A moment later, his lips touched mine and I parted them.

Chris slid his tongue deep into my mouth. I was glad I'd gargled three times. Having a bridge meant being extra careful with dental hygiene. He let go of my dick, I let go of his, and he hugged me tight against him as we continued kissing, making out for several more minutes. I felt his hands on my back, in my hair, on my nipples, and on my back again. I reached down to caress his ass.

Now it was his turn to moan. "I'll let you in there sometime if you like," he whispered before kissing me again.

"I can't wait," I murmured back. "Are you okay with flip fucking?"

"Mmm." Chris nuzzled my neck. "I like the way *you* give directions a whole lot better than that other guy."

"He who shall not be named if we don't want our dicks to go flaccid."

Chris chuckled and then reached in between our stomachs to grasp my dick again. He tried to draw things out as long as possible, but I could only last another five minutes. Soon I could feel my warmth spurting against both our bodies, grateful I could even cum at all. With my prostate medication, that wasn't always a given.

"Shall I finish you?" I whispered as he pulled away.

Chris shook his head and kept stroking himself. He was already well lubed but was now using my cum as additional lubricant. That was frowned on here. We were supposed to wipe up immediately to reduce the chance of infection. I was mesmerized, though, and couldn't tear my eyes away. When I did finally look up, his eyes locked onto mine. Then his face began to contort. His eyes squinched.

And then he shot up and out. Even standing more than a foot away, some of his cum hit my stomach.

I smiled and grabbed a paper towel to help clean him up. He pulled me close, pressing his cum-covered abdomen against mine and whispering his phone number into my ear. I repeated it and whispered mine back.

Chris gave me one last peck on the lips and then headed for the restroom to clean up. "Gotta get ready for round two." He winked. I didn't grab another paper towel just yet, basking in the afterglow as I watched three men next to me fondling each other.

Why anyone else should care what we did with our dicks was truly beyond my comprehension.

After another fifteen minutes, the room was packed with men. No new guests seemed to be arriving, and Chris's cum was beginning to dry on my skin. I decided I'd leave most of it there, wiping off just the part that was still wet. It was fun to ride light rail home, knowing I had another man's cum on my body.

I went to the restroom, washed my hands, peed, washed my hands again, and headed down to the basement. As I turned the corner at the bottom of the stairs, I groaned. Thank God I wasn't on clean-up crew yet. Men were pigs. Someone had spilled a bottle of juice or soda all over the floor. There was a reason unsupervised food and drink weren't allowed at these events.

Then I took another step and stopped. That wasn't juice. It was blood, and it was everywhere, fresh and glistening. A flash caught my eye where part of the knife that wasn't covered in blood reflected the overhead lighting.

And right smack dab in the center of the mess was a naked man flat on his back, something stuffed in his mouth, his throat slit, and his eyes frozen in horror.

Salvador Castro was dead.

Chapter Two

"Go get Clayton."

I held my hand up like a Stop sign to prevent a caramel-colored man from descending any farther. He frowned. "I'm getting dressed," he explained with no trace of an Indian accent. He pointed down the stairs past me.

"We need Clayton down here before *anyone* else can come."

The young man hesitated but must have sensed my determination. He turned and headed back up the stairs. Yes, I noticed his firm ass as he climbed to the main floor, but I certainly wasn't thinking about sex anymore.

There was so much blood in the locker room it didn't seem possible it all came from one person. I shivered, realizing the murder must have just happened. New arrivals had only stopped showing up a few minutes ago. Was the last arrival the murderer? Was the killer still here? What if he was hiding behind the New Member Orientation curtain?

I climbed up a step and kept looking behind me and then back upstairs and then back behind me again.

I knew Chris was irritated with Salvador, but he didn't seem mad enough even to shout at him, much less do anything else. And he was with me most of the time.

Salvador seemed not to have learned how to play well with others. Perhaps he'd never gone to kindergarten. Maybe Clayton would have an idea who might have done it. I'd heard him complaining the last time I volunteered about Salvador's insufferable attitude driving folks away. It's what had emboldened me to speak up earlier this evening after putting up with it every other time.

Clayton was a surprisingly fit sixty-year-old who headed JOB and usually kept the music and videos running smoothly. Sometimes, he remained clothed for the event and other times, he played. Tonight, fortunately, he was clothed.

When the attractive Indian returned with Clayton, I held up my hand once more to stop the naked man from reaching the bottom of the stairs, but I waved Clayton on with a small nod and tilt of my head. His brows furrowed as he slowed his pace and peeked around the corner.

"Fucking hell!"

Clayton hurried back to me. "Keep everyone out of here." He pointed then to the young Indian man. "Pranav, tell the reception crew to lock the doors and turn on the lights."

The young man didn't question the orders. He blinked rapidly a couple of times and then ran up the stairs.

I saw Clayton pull out his cell phone before I climbed to the main floor so no one else could even try to start down. I waved David over, a Mark Spitz lookalike who'd been monitoring the water and mints. Fortunately, he was dressed, too. Other than two of the guys in the reception area wearing jock straps, everyone else in the building was still naked.

"We have a situation in the basement," I told him. "Clayton's called for help."

"Help? You mean an ambulance? Someone had a heart attack?" David liked older men—other than me—and peered over my shoulder down the stairwell.

"No ambulance," I said.

I could see David's face grow pale even in the dim light as he understood. Pranav returned a moment later. "Anything else I can do?"

He wasn't circumcised, so probably Hindu. I wondered if gay Sikhs removed their head covering in sex clubs. Mormons were allowed to take off their special underwear for sex. Well, for *approved* sex. I still had a pair of the one-piece "garments" that I wore at the last Underwear Night event.

Unapproved sex, so I kept them on while another man beat me off through the slit in front and another man caressed me through the slit in back.

The lights suddenly brightened throughout the playroom, eliciting a roar of disapproval, like moviegoers interrupted during a screening of *The Rocky Horror Picture Show*. "Tell the guys at the check-in counter the police will be here soon, and then grab a linen. There won't be enough for everyone."

I didn't have one.

I wished I could take advantage of the Time Warp again.

I watched as Pranav grabbed a linen first and then headed back to the front of the building. Cool under pressure. Impressive. Meanwhile, I was dripping in sweat. It didn't help that the thermostat was adjusted to accommodate people without any clothes in early December and I felt hot even at normal temperatures. I'd actually considered wearing a kind of rubber crown Tommy had bought for my birthday, with two tiny fans attached and aimed down toward my face, but even at a Comic Con event, I'd look too alien for sex.

My brother had once accused me of being a lizard person. In all seriousness.

And right-wing Christians thought *we* were weird.

Jared and his wife were currently serving a senior LDS mission in Paraguay.

Chris, fully erect again, jumped off a padded bench and joined David and me at the top of the stairs. Rather than feel I had an in with other volunteers, I instead felt I'd be crossing a line to approach one during playtime, so tonight was the first time I'd managed to play with another volunteer despite helping out five times now. I wondered if the club would even be able to meet again after what had just happened.

I wondered why I was wondering about such a thing at a time like this.

"What's up?" Chris pointed to the ceiling lights with his thumb.

"Salvador's been murdered," I said, softly enough that only David and Chris could hear.

David gasped. Chris's expression didn't change.

"It looked like his mouth was stuffed with something," I went on. "Maybe a pair of underwear."

Chris's gaze pierced all the way through my eyes and into my soul. "I see."

I'd joked with Stu about an underwear gag, not Chris. So why did he act like he knew?

I couldn't find Stu in the crowd but pointed to Marin. "Help everyone find a linen that'll wrap about them. The police will be here any minute."

Sure enough, a few seconds later, we could hear sirens approaching. Chris hadn't even reached Marin yet when we heard banging on the front door. A moment later, several officers rushed in. No guns drawn, thank goodness. If they weren't expecting a mass shooting, though, why all the drama?

Many of the men in the room, already confused and irritated, ducked and darted about as if they'd been caught having sex with someone's husband. And with more gay cops on the force these days, maybe they had. Several of the guys tonight were even older than I was. Whether we'd personally been in a bar raid or not, we all knew folks who had.

Damn. Why hadn't I made some kind of announcement? Prepared everyone. Trying to prevent a panic had instead pushed some of the men closer to it.

You know that dream when you show up at school naked?

Remember playing musical chairs as a kid?

Combine those memories and you'll get some sense of the havoc in the playroom as men ripped linens off the furniture. The two tug-of-wars I witnessed might have been sexy under other circumstances. A few groups of three, four, even five men cooperated by wrapping the larger linens from the sofas and padded cube around them. But there still weren't enough to cover everyone. Marin stood behind a loveseat. If only the poor fellow weren't so tall. The few linens he'd managed to reach for had been too small and he'd passed them on to others.

Normally self-conscious even alone in my own bathroom, I felt as unconcerned now as when my doctor examined me.

If you ever need a cystoscopy, and your doctor says it might be "uncomfortable," believe him. And here's an added tip: it's very, very good to be flaccid during the procedure, so do *not* fantasize about your doctor.

The next couple of hours were a blur of boredom, terror, and confusion. I kept waiting for someone to offer me one of those gold foil blankets, but none came. And blood covered so much of the floor in front of the lockers that there was no way to let anyone get dressed until the forensics team had finished their work securing the crime scene, taping off the area, removing the body.

Inspecting every square inch of the locker room.

I'd only taken in the sight for half a minute before turning back up the stairs but would never forget the image. Some might have said tonight was like a horror movie, only it wasn't. Seeing a brutally murdered man, even one you disliked, was a life changing event. Like having my ceiling collapse during an earthquake in Italy. Like having sex for the very first time at the age of twenty-three with a classmate from my Cell Physiology class. Like being pulled into an alley and raped by two gay bashers after an ACT UP demonstration in the eighties.

1988, to be specific. October 6th. 4:37 p.m.

"Who found the body?"

Two detectives were on the scene now, a striking white man in his upper thirties and a black woman maybe a few years older. The woman, Detective Gwen Downey, seemed to be in charge. She wasn't quite trim but wasn't overweight by much, either, with medium-toned skin and shoulder-length hair in wavy rivulets. Loose curls? I didn't know the first thing about hair terminology.

I'd have made a bad drag queen.

The other detective's skin wasn't exactly swarthy but close enough to catch my interest. Detective Demir Altan had a five o'clock shadow and a narrow goatee like a vertical pencil moustache. It started with something less than a soul patch right under his lower lip, with a thin trail of nine o'clock shadow leading to his chin, followed by another tiny patch of beard there. Along with the narrow sideburns reaching past the bottom of his ears and his closely cropped hair, Detective Altan was calendar worthy.

I couldn't help but feel a ding on my gaydar over the stylish detective. He even had a tiny loop earring in his left ear.

I raised my hand. The detectives had already questioned Clayton, who'd explained that I'd been the one to find Salvador. Their question now was to determine which of the men milling about was me.

"Altan," I said, looking at the nametag. "Turkish?"

The detective raised an eyebrow.

I shrugged. "I'm a big Mehmet Günsür fan." As much for his Italian work as his Turkish.

I nodded to the lead detective to let her know I wasn't trying to ignore her authority, turning to her for the first question. I introduced myself and then explained what I'd seen. The detectives hadn't let me go back to the basement, but I hardly needed a refresher. I could still see the gaping neck wound, could still see the staring eyes.

"I realize I'll be one of the main suspects for a while," I said. "Several folks will be able to tell you I had an argument with Salvador this evening. He was a big S.O.B. And I know the person who finds a body is often a suspect anyway."

"Watch a lot of TV, do you, Mr. Chealander?" Detective Downey asked.

"*Annika Bengtzon, Detective Marleau, Carlo and Malik, Detective Montalbano, Homicide: Istanbul…*"

"We get the idea."

"My husband and I like European TV."

"Is he European?" Detective Altan asked. I saw Detective Downey give him a look.

"Duwamish." The only positive thing Tommy could say about having been raised LDS was that it gave him the chance to live in Peru for two years, even if he'd been "called" to preach to other "Lamanites" there.

He would never forgive the LDS church for its Indian Placement Program, though.

"I'd just had sex with Chris"—I pointed him out in the crowd—"watched a few other guys play, and then went downstairs." I'd already heard the reception area guys say no one had left the building in the ten minutes before they called 9-1-1. "I didn't see anyone walking away from the stairwell as I approached it."

"Did Mr. Castro have any enemies?" Detective Downey asked.

"At least one," I said.

She gave me the look she'd just given Detective Altan a moment earlier.

"Sorry. What I meant is I'm not going to say, 'Oh, everyone loved him.' I suppose some people might have liked him, but I can't imagine who those people are."

Detective Altan coughed and covered his mouth.

"Any former sex partners here?" Detective Downey asked.

I bit my tongue. "Um, probably," I managed.

"Salvador dated a couple dozen guys he met here," Clayton interjected. "He couldn't help but boast about it. But he did his 'dating' somewhere else since our club rules limit what we can do in this space."

Hmm, had Clayton changed his shirt since set-up? He did work with the lights, I remembered. That probably got pretty hot. Though he wasn't sweating now.

Damn if the man's calm self-assurance didn't make him sexy as hell. I wished I'd had the nerve to approach him on a night when he was playing. He'd uploaded one of his own jack off videos to the montage we watched.

Clayton was definitely *not* on prostate medication.

I'd personally never wanted a penis pump so much as I'd needed a semen catapult.

I had a sudden memory from an episode of *Buffy, the Vampire Slayer* where a spell gives Buffy the ability to hear the inner thoughts of her friends. She finally yells at Xander. "Is sex the only thing you think about?" Pretty much all men on some level were pigs, of course. It's what I liked best about them.

I refocused on the detectives.

"He was a dedicated volunteer," Clayton added, "but most of us could hardly stand the guy, so we didn't ask many questions, and we really don't keep tabs on each other, anyway." I caught the glance he shared with Detective Altan. "What happens at JOB stays at JOB, and what happens away from here is none of our business."

Had the two of them played before, I wondered? Was that glance an invitation? An assurance? Simply a recognition of brotherhood?

Despite watching TV mysteries and reading the occasional Greg Herren novel, I had no clue how detectives worked in the real world. For one thing, it struck me as odd they'd interviewed both me and Clayton in front of each other and everyone else. As they moved on to questioning the remaining JOB participants, the detectives continued to keep us all within earshot.

I mean, it was a big room, but still.

Of course, other than the restrooms, the kitchen crammed with equipment, and the basement covered with blood, there really weren't many other options. And without access to our clothes, we couldn't very well head down to the station. Besides, at this point, none of us were truly suspects, just witnesses, so there was no need yet for an official interview room.

But it still felt weird.

I suppose the detectives could have called for blankets to be brought in for us, though that seemed little better than the linens we already wore. I might have wondered if keeping us naked was intended as harassment except for Detective Altan's presence. It was still probably a breach of some sort.

But perhaps that was why we were being interviewed in front of each other rather than being pulled aside naked and out of sight.

I remembered reading once about a Hollywood actress filming a scene in her underwear who told the crew that her contract demanded everyone present also had to be in their underwear to avoid a power imbalance, and she waited until the crew all stripped down before she'd film the scene.

She'd been lying, of course, but did enjoy feeling slightly less objectified.

I wondered if I could ask Detective Altan to strip while he questioned us. But he might be one of those employees who actually read his union contract.

Howard, a fit Asian man about thirty-five, with a buzz cut moustache and a slightly longer goatee, admitted to arguing with Salvador at an event a couple of months earlier. "Then when I went to get dressed after playing with a guy that evening"—he glanced in Marin's direction—"I found that my locker had been broken into."

"And you suspected Mr. Castro?" Detective Downey asked.

Howard shrugged. "Mine was the only locker broken into. I've been coming here for over two years. It's never happened to anyone else before or since that I know of."

"So you're telling us you had a motive?" Detective Altan said.

"I could have followed him to his car later." Howard shrugged. "Written down his license plate and then slashed his tires on another night if I'd wanted revenge."

"Sounds like you considered it."

"Or walked by while he was jacking off with someone and made a withering remark." He stuck out his tongue and wiggled it. "I have quite the sharp tongue, I'm told."

Detective Altan coughed again, covering his mouth once more. I hoped he didn't have a cold. After four years of dealing with COVID fears, I found that one of the most irritating things someone could say when spreading infection was, "It's just a cold." Yeah, I don't want your damn cold, either. Mask up when you're sick. JOB posted a sign in the reception area: "Sniffles? Please come back another night."

Andrew, a guy about fifty, was the next to be questioned. I'd only seen him at JOB once before. Incision scars on his torso made me wonder if he'd had excess skin removed. He had one of those expressionless faces some men assumed when they felt that revealing any emotion at all wasn't appropriately masculine. The kind of man who'd never smile in a photo, afraid he wouldn't look butch enough. The type who wouldn't tell you he'd seroconverted, even though you were supposed to be in a monogamous relationship, and even though you weren't using condoms because you thought you were safe.

Okay. Maybe I was projecting a bit here. Scott hadn't been in my life for many, many years now. It was just that some wounds left surprisingly thick scars.

"Salvador and I used to be partners," Andrew said.

Oh my god. He *was* an ex! His cold face almost made me feel sympathy for Salvador for the first time. Unless Andrew had grown cold *because* of his time with the man.

"We broke up ten years ago," Andrew went on. "I only started coming here three weeks ago. I hadn't seen Sal in a long time."

"Was your breakup amicable?" Detective Altan asked.

"He cheated on me."

"You didn't answer my question."

"I burned his address book before I left."

Detective Altan and Detective Downey both wrote something down.

The evening dragged on. Most of the men didn't have much to say, so each interview only lasted a couple of minutes. But with sixty men, that still added up. Tuyen said he overheard two men saying "mean things" about Salvador, but he couldn't remember the specific wording and wouldn't single out who'd made those comments, explaining it was too dark to see clearly. Jelani said he saw Salvador in the corridor near the bathroom thrusting his finger in someone's face, but the other guy was on the far side of Salvador, so Jelani didn't get a good look at him.

"I think he was white, though," he said.

Freddie said he saw Salvador scowl and bare his teeth at an Asian man who approached him.

At a certain point, I could no longer guess who was telling the truth and who wasn't. Perhaps one of them was trying to divert suspicion by making things up.

The questioning went on so long I could see a group of five men who were sharing a large linen start fondling each other as they waited for their interview. Did that behavior prove anything about them one way or the other? Were four of those guys genuinely bored and horny and the fifth intentionally going along so as not to single himself out?

I expected we were all a bit worried about being outed for playing at a sex club. Perhaps our partners didn't care where we were, but our bosses and coworkers and neighbors might.

Finally, after enough evidence had been documented, men were allowed to enter the locker room six at a time, under supervision as they opened their lockers and dressed. At least the last few attendees were clothed during their interviews. Officers had searched the rest of the building during the questioning and found no one hiding, nothing that looked suspicious.

Tommy would be wondering why I was so late. As soon as I could get to my phone, I'd give him a call. Still, I wasn't anxious to return to the locker room yet. I let the other men go first.

Detective Downey spoke again with Clayton while Detective Altan moved over toward me. "I take it you're a grower?" he said casually, rubbing the little tuft of hair on his chin.

"Excuse me?"

"And not a show-er?"

Really? Was he serious? "Those are options A and B," I said. "You didn't give me an option C. And you forgot D. 'None of the above.'"

He laughed, and for the first time in hours, I felt a weight lift off my chest. I made a melodramatic show of searching for my penis among my pubic hairs, generating another chuckle from the detective. "This has been worse than the coldest shower I ever took."

Tommy and I talked often about taking an Alaskan cruise to look at glaciers before they all melted, but we'd never done it.

"You gonna be okay?" the detective asked. "That was a pretty gruesome sight." His eyes were focused on my stomach, and at first, I wondered if he was making a passive aggressive comment about my weight. I wasn't fat, but I did have a granddad bod.

Then I realized he was looking at Chris's dried cum. I shook my head. "I watch a German show called *Crime Scene Cleaner*," I told him. "It's a comedy."

He raised an eyebrow.

"The blood doesn't bother me," I said. "It was his face. I'm never going to forget his face."

Detective Altan handed me a card. "Here's my number. Call me if you remember anything," he said.

I nodded.

"And call me if you need to get hooked up with some counseling."

The "hooked up" phrasing threw me for a second, making me pause. I couldn't pocket the card just yet, still waiting for my turn downstairs, but I studied the number and nodded again. "Thanks."

The detective looked over his shoulder and then back at me, clapping a hand on my upper arm and giving it a squeeze. "And when the investigation is over," he said, "give me a call anyway."

Now it was my turn to laugh. The man had seen me at my least attractive. I should take that to mean that when I was looking better, I must look pretty good indeed. But instead, I said, "Are you sure *you're* not the one who needs counseling?" I motioned toward my chest and groin, jiggled the loose skin on my neck.

"Nope," he said. "None of that. You wouldn't put up with a friend of yours saying that about someone else. Don't put up with you saying it, either." He shook his head. "I want you to call me."

Even though I'd always liked older guys, it was hard to believe other men sometimes did, too.

Our eyes locked, and I felt something. Not sexual interest necessarily, maybe not even an offer of friendship. But connection. I felt a *connection*, in a dysfunctional society that made such things all but impossible. It was really the main reason I came to these events in the first place. Hoping for a chance to feel what I'd just felt.

It felt good.

Given the situation, it also felt somewhat inappropriate. But I didn't care.

"Thanks," I said again. "I will."

"Now let's get you downstairs and into some clothes."

I sure wish I'd worn a more stylish shirt.

Chapter Three

Tommy was asleep by the time I got home. He hadn't answered my texts or even my phone call after I was finally able to retrieve my cell. I figured he was pissed, thinking maybe I was spending the night with another guy. Even if we had an open relationship and no longer enjoyed sex as a couple, sleepovers broke the rules.

But he'd gone to bed, mad or not I didn't know. I disrobed again, feeling far more vulnerable now than I had in front of all the police officers and detectives, and took a quick shower. Then I snuggled up behind Tommy as the big spoon.

I felt tempted to pry open his cheeks and press my way in. But while I'd given him advance permission to fuck me in my sleep, he hadn't returned the invitation. The few times other partners had entered me in the middle of the night, I'd loved waking up knowing I was making them happy. It was unfortunate Tommy never took me up on the offer. Our most significant sexual incompatibility was that he liked sex most between the hours of 11:00 p.m. and 1:00 a.m. while I liked sex better at almost any other time—middle of the night up until about 9:00 p.m.

In our Venn diagram, the circles didn't overlap.

People think sexual compatibility means frequency or sexual positions. No one thinks about the time of day.

I wrapped my arm around Tommy's chest, and he sighed. I did, too.

This long, horrible nightmare was over. I might be questioned again, but my part was essentially complete. I was safely away from whoever had killed Salvador, and maybe if I did call Detective Altan to get access to a therapist, life could return to relative normality quickly. If the police never figured out who the murderer was, it was none of my business, any more than seeking justice for all the other horrific things that happened every day.

Like that poor bus driver who'd been pulled off his bus in the U District the other day and stabbed to death in an alley.

However awful Salvador was, he didn't deserve to be murdered. But I still wouldn't be attending his funeral.

***

"Bruce!"

I felt hands batting me about and tried to fight back.

"Bruce!"

My eyes opened. All I saw was darkness as I continued to struggle against my attacker. The murderer had followed me home!

"Bruce! Bruce!"

I slowly stopped struggling. That was Tommy's voice. I was in bed with Tommy. My heart rate began to slow, though I was still panting like a dog.

"What the hell?" Tommy had my arms pinned down. "You don't have nightmares." He was the one who had occasional dreams about the day he was taken from his home and placed with a good Mormon family to help assimilate him into white culture.

"Hold me."

Tommy lay back down and became the big spoon now, his arms wrapped tightly around me. I pressed his arms even more tightly against my chest.

I loved cuddling pretty much any time, and even back when we had sex regularly, there was a time for sex and a time for cuddling. But when all we shared these days was the cuddling, it was difficult sometimes not to want physical intimacy to morph into sexual. It was like being at a concert of your favorite musician and forced to stick your fingers in your ears and shout, "La la la la la!" all through the music to keep yourself from hearing what you loved.

Having permission to engage in sex with other guys if we wanted didn't mean that gay men didn't choose to exercise self-control. Tommy had set boundaries and I loved him, so I lived with the boundaries.

I told Tommy what happened at Jack Off Buddies while he held me. He listened quietly until the end. I was the one who sometimes had to be careful not to interrupt people. One of my mantras was WAIT—Why Am I Talking? Even if I had something interesting to say (debatable) or wanted to ask a clarifying question, I'd trained myself over the years to wait before speaking.

Most of the time.

"You shouldn't go back until they catch whoever did this."

I sighed heavily, pressing Tommy's arms more tightly against my chest.

"What?"

"Hook up sites are almost useless," I said. "Guys either don't respond at all or they agree to meet but then the instant you ask for a time and place, they ghost you."

"You can survive without sex for a few months."

True enough, I supposed. In fact, for the past several years before I discovered JOB, I usually only had sex two or three times a year, at best maybe one of those times with Tommy. The COVID pandemic sure hadn't helped. It was just that with the recent election, the future felt less predictable than usual. It never truly was, of course, but these MAGA folks had campaigned on anti-LGBTQ hate, and they were quite good at being awful. Things were *not* going to stay the same. We'd either go back to some form of Jim Crow against all marginalized groups, when oral and anal sex, even for heterosexual married couples, were felonies.

Or conditions might get even worse than that.

We could face an anti-LGBTQ propaganda law like Russia had. No more books or movies with queer characters. No more online forums or YouTube channels. No bars or community centers. No Netflix or Hulu shows that acknowledged our existence. Nothing.

What if even the possession of such material became criminalized? The government could already confiscate personal property if it was "involved" in the commission of a crime. Cars, boats, and planes were the properties most often seized, even when the owners weren't the actual criminals, but if housing gay books became a crime, and you housed them in your home, would thousands of us face the theft of our homes?

That couldn't *really* happen, could it? Not *here*.

Everyone knew that homes, businesses, and artwork were stolen from the Jews. Japanese Americans lost their property, too. And almost all indigenous property had been stolen. Permanently.

Tommy was the one who'd explained the double theft of Fort Lawton to me.

While blacklists against communists ended just about the time we were born, Tommy and I had both reached high school before the lavender scare ended.

Both of us had been raised Mormon. We *knew* how obsessed with policing the morality of others Christian nationalists and "law and order" conservatives could be.

My brother had a fit when he saw Michelle Obama wearing a sleeveless dress. "The hussy!"

Now the LDS church produced sleeveless garments for women. But non-Mormons were still sinners regardless.

"Maybe they'll find the guy quickly," Tommy said.

I might want to call Detective Altan, after all. Not only for a therapist referral but to get a sense of how the investigation was going. Perhaps he couldn't give me specifics, but even a hint of whether this was a one-off or part of a serial killing would go a long way in easing tension.

Maybe I could piggyback emotional trauma therapy with discussing my anxiety over the future and get in a few free sessions.

"Let's get back to sleep," Tommy suggested. "We've got a couple more hours before we need to get ready for work." He gently pushed me away and kept pushing until I lay on my stomach. Then he climbed on top, pried my legs apart, and lay down on my back, his flaccid dick tickling my balls.

He was a show-er.

Tommy knew I liked to feel the weight of another man on me, but at our age, neither of us could risk sleeping on our backs. Even moderate sleep apnea was a bitch. Some nights, I slept sitting up on the sofa. But one prone man on top of another worked just fine.

Tommy kissed my neck and pulled the covers over us. "Goodnight, Bruce." He kissed me again. "I love you."

Chapter Four

Work, as always, was something to be endured. Not awful, not physically painful or exhausting, but a waste of my remaining time on Earth. Cashiers at the county courthouse filled a useful function. Pretty much every job in society filled a useful function or it wouldn't exist.

Well, pretty much everything except middle management.

But four hours into a shift, I was ready to come home. Only the shift kept dragging on. Five hours, six hours, seven hours, eight hours. That, plus lunch, plus the commute there, plus the commute home, and I suddenly had an eleven- to twelve-hour day.

I'd cut down to four days a week, but neither Tommy nor I could afford to take Social Security. My monthly check would be a little over $1100. His would be slightly more than $1200. Tommy had another year before he could start receiving his payments without penalty. I had a year and a half.

And even with my Social Security check, I'd need to keep working. I might, though, be able to drop down to three days a week. That was probably as good as it was ever going to get. I'd be working until the day I died.

As had Salvador.

With the far right trying to destroy Social Security altogether, I might never be able to deposit even a single check. I was Charlie Brown trying to kick Lucy's football, only I couldn't kick until after running a full marathon first.

And the ball might *still* be yanked away.

It wasn't even that I had plans to fill my days if I was ever able to retire completely. I just wanted my time to be mine. Tommy and I could take more walks together, play Scrabble a little more often, maybe go to a physical movie theater to watch a film, eat at a restaurant without worrying we needed to hurry home and sleep so we'd be alert the next morning at work.

So I did my job Thursday, I did it with a smile and, as usual, I balanced to the penny at the end of my shift.

During my lunch break, I texted Chris from last night. It was awkward to pursue sex after all that, but if too many days passed without following up on the phone number he'd given me, it would feel even more awkward to finally reach out.

"Want to meet up?" I asked.

"Yes. I'm fucking Stu tonight. You want to fuck me tomorrow night?"

"Yes."

Chris asked for my address, said he'd stop over around 7:00, and sent me a picture of his asshole. I replied with a tongue emoji. He replied with an eggplant emoji. I replied with a clapping hands emoji.

Then I finished eating my sandwich and returned to my post.

Tommy cooked dinner when he got home. I sent out the weekly email to SILT (Solidarity Is Labor Together), a small group of labor advocates here in Seattle. Union organizers were holding a practice picket at a major coffee chain this Sunday on Capitol Hill. We sent our endorsement to support striking Canadian postal workers. And we needed to start making plans for a meeting in early January so we'd be ready to rally on MLK Day. Which would also be Inauguration Day.

Uffa.

Tommy and I watched *Portrait Artist of the Year* as we ate, and then we held hands on the sofa for the next episode of *Tatort:Vienna*. I loved Bibi, though I was always afraid she might start drinking again.

***

"Thanks for making the drive out here," I said, giving Chris a kiss as he came into the house Friday evening. "South Seattle's quite a trek from Ballard."

He nipped my ear and shrugged. "I like driving. Gives me time to think."

"Well, I sure hope you got *that* out of the way." I closed the door and directed him toward the bedroom. "I have better plans for this evening." I was trying not to let my dependence on public transit keep me from living the life I wanted, but even heading to Columbia City, a neighborhood relatively nearby, could take close to an hour. It was almost faster to walk.

An hour to get there, an hour spent there, an hour to get back, and I'd have spent three hours of my evening after work or of my day off on just a few minutes of social interaction. So that interaction really had to count. Yet putting that much pressure on a social interaction almost guaranteed it wouldn't measure up.

Damn. Now *I* was thinking too much. I needed to channel my inner airhead if I wanted to feel sexy tonight.

"Let's get naked," I said. Tommy had dinner with friends almost every Friday evening and wouldn't return for another couple of hours. Plenty of time to explore Chris's body.

There's no need to get into the nitty gritty of the next forty-five minutes. TLDR: We kissed, we blew each other for a bit, we kissed and rolled around on the bed for a while, and then I fucked him and he fucked me. Chris asked me to wear a condom, which I did. I asked him not to wear one, and he didn't.

Then it was time for afterglow. Chris lay on my back, still inside me, nuzzling my neck.

"I fucked Stu yesterday."

I'd wanted to follow up on his adventures after Chris told me about his plans, but I didn't want to overstep. "Fun?" I asked. Always hard to navigate nosiness with showing interest in another person's life.

"I got to play Ace Ventura." Chris pumped playfully against my ass.

"You did some detecting?"

"Doggy style. It let me assume a dominant stance when I asked why he left so early Wednesday night."

"Oh?" I could feel Chris growing flaccid inside me before he pulled out gently.

"He said he'd gone down to the locker room to put away his watch and ran into Salvador."

We both grabbed hand towels and wiped lube off ourselves. Then Chris leaned back against some pillows, his legs spread out.

"Want a picture?" he asked, giving me a wink.

I grabbed my phone and snapped a couple of shots.

"So what happened in the locker room?" I asked.

"Stu said Salvador made fun of him. Told Stu, and I quote, 'It must be true about old people shrinking. You're the same height as always, but your dick gets shorter every time I see you.'"

"That's a very long quote."

"It seemed to have left an impression on the guy."

I thought about my zone leader in Rome, who used to pop into the bathroom while I was showering to make sure I wasn't sinning. One day, as he pulled back the shower curtain, he'd said, in complete disgust, "I bet you don't even know *how* to masturbate."

He'd gone on to become a gynecologist after his mission. And a bishop.

"What happened then?" I asked.

"He says he told Sal, and I quote again. 'At least you can still see my dick. Your heart is so tiny you're going to die of a heart attack.'"

"He doesn't watch much drag, does he?" A better line might have been, "so tiny even Raquel Welch couldn't fit inside," but I suppose you really needed to know your Raquel Welch movies to get the reference.

Chris shrugged. "I expect that was something he came up with after the fact. And since that wasn't much of a zing, I expect what he actually said was even less of one."

"Was that the end of the argument?"

"So he says." Chris got up on his hands and knees, his ass toward me, and let me take a few more pictures. "Stu said he didn't see anyone else down there. He decided not to go back up and play. He just got dressed and left. Said it looked like Salvador was waiting for someone."

"You think he was telling the truth?"

Chris shrugged once again. It was almost like a wink, playful, inviting. I was way too old for a second round, of course. I was lucky I'd stayed hard enough to get inside him as it was. Even with a dick pill, that wasn't a given.

He stood now and began pulling on his clothes. "I'm heading to Marin's place now," he said.

"Ah, to be young again."

"I know it sounds weird, but I'm taking an online course for private investigators." He lowered his gaze and hid his face. Coy was not a natural look for him. And there was no way he was embarrassed.

"That's great."

"Feels pretentious somehow. As if I could ever really be good at something like that."

Now it was my turn to shrug. "You won't know unless you try."

Chris looked up and smiled. "Thanks."

That had almost felt rehearsed, which seemed odd. But maybe this was how he told everyone about his studies. Chris wore confidence like a second skin, but appearing confident wasn't always the same thing as feeling it.

Fake it 'til you make it. But I often had to fake faking it as well, or I'd have no chance at all.

I got dressed too and led him to the door. "I hope we can play again," he said. "JOB is great fun, but there are things I like that I can't do there."

"So I've noticed."

"I have a few more things I'd like to try with you."

"Send me some emoji hints?" I asked.

He grinned and batted his eyes. "Two eggplants?"

Hmm. A dildo and a dick at the same time? Or was he bringing a friend? "So…next Friday?" A week to fantasize about possibilities.

On Valentine's Day in 2020, as it had become clear the pandemic was about to descend upon us, I'd given Tommy a card with a photo of a nude man riding a horse bareback, and listing 10 different sexual scenarios inside. We'd need to rely solely on each other for the foreseeable future. Two weeks later, we tried out the first scenario. Two more weeks passed, and then two months, before we tried out another. Then Tommy put the card away and my right hand became my primary sex partner once more.

Sometimes, I switched things up by using my left hand.

Chris smiled again. "It's a date."

He kissed me and headed out. Then I picked up the towels and washcloths and remade the bed. If Tommy wanted me to change the sheets, I would, but we had no trouble sleeping in sexually experienced bedclothes. I got Tommy's coffee ready to go for the morning, got his oatmeal ready for a bedtime snack later tonight, and then sat on the sofa to listen to music while watching a video of crashing waves along the Oregon coast.

I wasn't sure which had been more satisfying, sex with a fun forty-year-old or the vicarious thrill when Chris told me about his amateur investigation.

Both had felt good, to be honest.

The only other phone number for a possible hook up I'd ever gotten at JOB was for Greg. We'd tried to meet up twice, but something always got in the way. I'd decided he wasn't that into me but thought now he might be worth one more call. Greg had been at the event the night Salvador was murdered, and it couldn't hurt to get any thoughts he might not have felt comfortable telling the detectives.

And the man did have a nice cock, lovely even soft. Maybe he'd let me take a few pictures, too.

I pulled out my phone and sent a text. Two songs later, he replied. I texted back, he replied again, and before long, I had another date. Tomorrow at 10:00 a.m. In SeaTac but within walking distance of the light rail station, he promised.

Taking more control of my life was fun. Why in the world had it taken me so long to start?

Chapter Five

Greg was right. His condo was barely a ten-minute walk from the SeaTac light rail station. The only problem was passing so many homeless folks milling about, digging through trash, holding up signs asking for food, or arguing with people only they could see, their breath turning into puffs of fog in the cold.

I could feel fear at the same time I felt compassion. Unpredictability was unnerving.

Things hadn't always been this way, so they didn't need to stay this way. Tommy and I and most of our friends were still reeling from the election results last month. Democratic elites blamed progressives. Progressives blamed corporate Democrats. Socialists blamed capitalists.

The bottom line was that Democrats hadn't delivered on what people needed. Republicans hadn't, either. But the whiny old man who'd won promised something radically different. Fascism. The truth was that desperate people were willing to try anything, like a terminally ill patient enrolling for a study using a dangerous, experimental drug.

The problem was that we *knew* what this drug was going to do.

"You found the place okay?" Greg asked when he opened the door.

"Your directions were perfect."

He ushered me inside. His living room was pristine, not a speck of dust anywhere. Something I think I'd accomplished once in 1997. The mantle over a fake fireplace displayed family photos in sleek, modern frames. Lots of kids and grandkids, I assumed, or various niblings.

Greg led me to his bedroom, his bedclothes pulled back neatly, folded hand towels ready for us on both bedside tables. I felt odd being here instead of with Tommy, like I was living with a chef but never eating at home, always needing to grab a sandwich somewhere on the run.

But when you were hungry…

I'll gloss over the next twenty minutes. Greg let me know he couldn't get hard, even with pills, but still loved to have his dick sucked. So I sucked his flaccid cock for twenty minutes. He didn't want to blow me after I told him I was poz but did offer to give me a hand job. I declined, saying I'd use my rain check at the next JOB event the following Saturday.

"Speaking of JOB," I said, ever so smoothly, "can I ask you some questions about last Wednesday?"

"Second worst day of my life."

I could hardly ask the obvious question, but he answered it anyway.

"The worst was the night my wife died."

"That must have been awful," I agreed, not knowing what else to say. But his comment left me confused. While seeing Salvador's slit throat had been horrific, it didn't rank in the Top 10 of terrible days in my own life.

There'd been my mother's death. The day I was excommunicated and learned that all the church members I'd believed genuine friends were in fact not. There was the day I seroconverted. Seeing my neighbors' bodies pulled out of their apartment in Napoli after the earthquake. Watching a Black Lives Matter protester two feet from me deliberately struck by a car.

Watching the January 6 insurrection live on television.

Really, the list was quite long. Salvador was on it, but he wasn't second.

Had Greg truly lived such a charmed life? "Did you know Salvador well?"

"We played some at his place. He's the guy who outed me to Marjolaine."

I paused, trying to keep my expression blank. Had Greg just given me a motive? He'd almost certainly kept that information to himself the night of the questioning. I hadn't overheard everyone, but that sounded like news which would have gotten around.

"She already knew, of course. I'd never told her outright, but she wasn't stupid. She handled the 'revelation' just fine, but Sal couldn't have known that. He thought he was going to force me out of the closet for my own good."

"You kept coming back to JOB after that?"

"I wanted to talk to Sal about my wife while I stroked myself next to him."

I barked out a laugh.

Greg smiled. "I know it was petty, but I liked to tell any other guys near us that Sal was the reason I couldn't get hard. Then I'd walk off 'in search of higher levels of testosterone.'"

I laughed again.

"Now that Sal's dead, I feel like I lost another connection to my wife." He sighed softly and closed his eyes. "I love the kids, but I don't see them much. Too far away."

Greg directed me back to the living room, where we spent another twenty minutes as he explained who everyone in the photographs was. I felt a tiny pang, as I often did in these situations, knowing I'd never see my family again.

But you couldn't reconcile with cruelty.

"Would you like to come to our place and watch a movie sometime?" I asked. "Tommy and I have a lot of DVDs." It was important to have physical copies of any work that could disappear the instant a streaming executive cut it off. I'd mailed over sixty gay movies to LGBTQ archives in other countries for safekeeping. If it turned out we didn't have fascism after all, those archives would still benefit from the donations.

Greg smiled. "I'd love to," he said.

We hugged at the door, and then I made my way back to the light rail station. An Asian man missing half his front teeth asked for spare change as I passed a convenience store. I didn't have any small bills but watched as a tall, stately trans woman in red exited the store, opened her purse shaped like a T-rex, and handed him a dollar.

Light rail from the terminal at Angle Lake all the way to a block before Rainier Beach was elevated, and for a long stretch, there were no stops at all, so the train zipped along quickly. But half a mile past Tukwila, the cars lurched to a halt.

Then the lights went out. Under the gray skies, the train grew dark.

A few minutes later, the conductor made an announcement. "We're experiencing a temporary power outage," she said. "We'll be moving again shortly."

I looked off to the left and watched traffic whiz by on the freeway. Some of the other riders near me grumbled about the delay, but I had nowhere I needed to be. The lack of urgency was refreshing. Almost every day could be like this, I realized, if I was retired.

I pulled out my phone and texted Tommy. "You up for a game of Scrabble this afternoon?"

He texted back a moment later. "You OK with me winning again?"

"Always."

In the twenty-five years we'd been playing, I might have won maybe three times. I wished I could say he cheated, but the truth was that he was both strategic and smart, an awful combination. And one of the many reasons I loved him.

I looked about at the other passengers on light rail. Several had suitcases, having boarded at SeaTac. Others looked dressed for a ballgame. I could never keep track of who was playing and where. But God forbid boarding just before or after a game. More tightly packed than a Napoletan bus.

An olive-skinned man scowled at an Asian woman eating a juicy piece of fruit that dripped onto the floor. Two teen girls with sparkly nails chatted happily, unconcerned about the delay. A young black man continued reading his book. I couldn't quite make out the title, though, darn it.

There were almost forty people in this car. Did any of them hold terrible secrets, I wondered? Was anyone here a murderer? I'd almost certainly seen a murderer last Wednesday and not noticed anything suspicious. I couldn't go about my life afraid to interact with everyone, but that didn't mean it wasn't creepy knowing there was an actual murderer in my circle.

I felt the way I had when Tommy and I had returned from a trip to the Hoh rainforest a few years earlier and discovered someone had broken into the house. Violated.

A few minutes later, the power came back on in the car. During that brief delay, a light drizzle had begun falling. By the time I stepped off at Rainier Beach, the drizzle had turned to rain. I jogged half a block to the bus shelter to wait for the 106. The next one wasn't due for another fifteen minutes.

Odd, I thought, how many people at JOB had a motive. People didn't merely dislike Salvador. They had reasons to loathe him.

Could his killing have been a *Murder on the Orient Express* kind of thing? Perhaps one man had held his arms while another stuffed his mouth and a third cut him.

Too horrific to think about.

Why was I thinking about it?

Because it wasn't *right*. With Christian extremists targeting LGBTQ folks more and more, we had to stand up for each other, even the jerks among us.

I knew one more phone number for another JOB member. Did I dare call Clayton? I only had his number because we'd needed to coordinate one of my volunteer sessions. I could check in just to see how he was coping, casually ask for any updates, get a feel for what to ask next.

Maybe I should call Chris for some guidance. Watching *Rockford Files* as a kid hadn't taught me any useful skills other than how to fantasize about James Garner without letting anyone around me know.

I trusted the police to do their job and *didn't* trust myself to do it. I didn't trust that Chris was up to the task, either. At least, not until he finished his studies. But I was curious. Nothing like this had ever happened so close to me before.

And my visit with Greg had proven there was some information the police might not be able to get on their own.

"Are you free to talk?" I texted Clayton.

He replied, "Sure," just as the 106 turned the corner from MLK. I punched the green telephone icon and didn't board when the bus opened its doors.

"I meant to thank you for all your help Wednesday night," Clayton said when he picked up. "Excuse my bad manners."

I laughed. "I expect you had plenty of other things on your mind."

"What a disaster."

"Are Salvador's family suing or anything?" I wasn't sure there'd be any legal justification for a lawsuit, but that wasn't always relevant.

I heard a loud sigh over the phone. "No one even wants to claim his body."

I did the gay gasp.

"I went ahead and paid for his cremation after the police released the body."

I reviewed the information Chris had given me plus what I'd learned this morning and asked Clayton if he had anything new to add.

"I spoke with Howard the next day," Clayton said. I vaguely remembered the man who'd had his locker broken into. "Turns out he had $200 in his wallet."

Still didn't seem like a terribly substantial motive.

"And the phone number of a guy he'd met on his way to JOB. Someone he wouldn't be able to contact now."

That didn't seem like a reason to kill, either. A reason to switch out someone's bottle of lube with superglue, perhaps, but not murder.

I shuddered, remembering the torturous story a guy had told me once on a first—and definitely last—date. "Have you had a chance to talk to anyone else?" I asked.

"I had Casey over last night, but his mouth was full pretty much the whole time, so not much talking."

I wasn't sure all gay men thought of sex as much as we did (or if all straight or bi men did, either). Even I didn't often think about specific sex acts. It was usually more like recognizing the smell of petrichor during a neighborhood walk and enjoying it. If I was watching someone giving a lecture, I might think, "Oh, he looks fun" or "I'd like to see the back of his head close up" or "Not sure but I'd definitely like to give him a try."

Of course, I could also discuss film technique with a friend, could enjoy a blustery day on my back deck, but I wasn't blind. I could appreciate a beautiful man every bit as much as I could stop and smell the lilac I passed on my way to the light rail station.

Male beauty was a part of nature to be celebrated.

"How about you?" Clayton asked.

"Um…"

Was being distracted so easily a sign of aging?

"I looked you up. You reported a break-in at a synagogue in your neighborhood last year. And you reported a homeless man who'd frozen to death back in February."

A block from the courthouse.

"Yeah?"

"I'm wondering if you're like a firebug."

"Excuse me?"

"Someone who sets fires and then reports them to feel a sense of importance."

I wasn't sure that was the definition of firebug, but I understood his point. "You think I killed Salvador so I could feel important when the police came?"

"I'm just saying."

"Uh huh." And did he pass that analysis on to the detectives, too?

"So…want to come over sometime?"

Okay, *sometimes* gay men were weird.

Chapter Six

Tommy had the Scrabble board set up by the time I walked through the door. He turned on the CD player—yes, we're old—and we started listening to Chris Housman. I gave Tommy a brief report on the morning's activities, and then we got down to business.

I picked the tile with the highest value and so made the first play. "M-U-R-D-E-R." I suppose it was inevitable the thought would be on my mind.

"Too bad you didn't have an S," Tommy said. The fact that he instantly added "O-U-S" to my word made me doubt his sincerity.

We chatted a bit about the news while we played. The president-elect was suggesting all sorts of horrible appointees, ambassadors, and cabinet members, people who'd for years spoken of their goal to destroy the EPA and Department of Education and almost every other essential government agency.

"He wants a far-right extremist to lead Voice of America," Tommy said.

Chris Housman began singing "Drag Queen."

Tommy spelled "Q-Ǝ-L-B," deliberately placing the "E" upside down. He didn't often throw Lushootseed words on the board, but I'd learned long ago not to challenge them. He was always accurate, and since he let me use Italian if I wanted, it evened out for the most part. Tommy was already 60 points ahead, so it wasn't as if he needed to squeeze in a few more. He just liked playing words he knew when he could.

I spelled "C-A-P-E," getting a triple letter score for my E, which gave me a whopping extra two points. Tommy instantly added "E-S" to the front of my word.

"I'll have another batch of watercolors for you tomorrow," he said.

While Tommy's work wasn't going to hang in many galleries, he was certainly above average. We'd framed his best work, a depiction of me on my knees admiring Tommy's cock, and hung it in the bedroom. Over the years, Tommy had gifted similar work to some of our friends. This past year, though, we'd mailed two dozen pieces of his original artwork to LGBTQ archives in Canada, Australia, Germany, Sweden, and The Netherlands. I'd even mailed a couple of pieces from other artists that I'd purchased years ago, homoerotic work by Skip Bailey and Ego Rodriguez.

Our walls weren't bare these days, but they were sparse. It was a matter of balancing preservation with deprivation. I simply couldn't stand the thought of MAGA enforcers burning books and artwork they deemed "dangerous." We couldn't know the specific awfulness just around the corner, only that it *would* be awful.

Even if it somehow didn't turn out to be as bad as the Cultural Revolution in China or the Holocaust in Europe, that didn't change what we were all feeling *now*, not knowing but hearing their threats. And the glee with which they delivered them.

We might not all be rounded up or killed, but genocide included cultural eradication, too. Tommy didn't lose all sense of his people after years with a white LDS family, but he'd had to struggle for whatever connection he did still feel, and it was more intellectual now than lived.

He could be grateful he wasn't sent to an Indian Boarding School as some of his relatives had been, but that was like being grateful for one broken leg instead of two.

So I'd also mailed queer books to some of the archives, plus CDs, T-shirts, and various pieces of ephemera—theater programs, gay newsletters, posters, and fliers. Donating gave me a sense of purpose when I spent most of my time feeling powerless.

"Let's be sure to take some good pictures of it all first," I said.

"Already done."

We chatted about the recent flooding in Spain, the workers washed away when Hurricane Helene hit Appalachia, and the wildfires in California. About the winning president's plan to take over Greenland and the Panama Canal, using force "if necessary."

I put "P-O-N-Y" on the board, and Tommy added "T-A-I-L," getting a double word score.

I put "J-U-N-K" on the board, and he added "E-T."

I put "B-R-I-S" on the board, and Tommy added "H-U" to the front.

"Damn, you're good," I said.

"That's what all the guys tell me."

There was an awkward silence for a few moments until I finally said, "I wish you could find some playmates, even if you don't want me as one of them."

"You aren't the only man who has a hard time getting your mouth over the head of it."

Chris Housman began singing, "Guilty as Sin."

It was a shame blow jobs were Tommy's favorite form of sex. Try as I might, I could never service such a huge object without scraping him with my teeth. It was terrible to know you couldn't deliver sexually for your partner. Suggesting he play with others always felt too much like a cop-out.

That plus our time preferences made our attempts too daunting.

"I need to go to the gym more first."

While there might be some value to delayed gratification, I no longer believed that delayed living was something to strive for.

Tommy put "R-A-B-B-I" on the board, and I added a "T," raising my fist in triumph.

Then he added "I-N-G" to the end.

"Damn, you're good."

"That's what all the guys tell me."

Twenty minutes later, the final score was 310 to 227. We didn't spend nearly enough time together just having fun, so when we did, I felt both relieved and a bit lonely, knowing how long it might be before we did something like this again.

And it appeared Tommy must have been feeling something similar. After I put the game away, he called me over to the sofa, patting the cushion beside him. "I think we need a Companion Inventory."

Never good words to hear, but I was grateful anyway. Despite our religious trauma, we'd retained one positive habit from our missionary days. Back then, whenever we'd had problems with our assigned companions, we'd hold a Companion Inventory to air our grievances and work toward a solution. Those sessions could be awkward or painful, yet being able to say the words "Companion Inventory" now sent an instant signal to stop everything and pay attention to the issue.

Tommy and I both came from families that chose to ignore problems. We'd committed from the start to keep an open line of communication.

"What are you feeling?" I asked, taking a deep breath as I sat down. It was hard to ask a question you weren't sure you wanted an answer to.

"Two things," he said. "One, I'm worried you're spending time alone with guys who might be the murderer at your club. And two, while I'm happy you're bonding with other men, I want to make sure you stay bonded to me, too." He squeezed my thigh. "Thank you for the Scrabble."

I nodded. Tommy's assessment was fair enough on both counts. I was more surprised by his first point, though, than his second. I hadn't seen the situation in those terms. It somehow never occurred to me that a suspect might change his classification and become a killer. It had felt like whoever slit Salvador's throat wouldn't be a murderer until he was arrested. *Then* he'd change categories in my mind.

"What would you like to do?" I asked, taking Tommy's hand and giving it a squeeze.

"If you were courting me again, what would you suggest?"

I'd heard Tommy mention a craving last week we hadn't acted on. Cravings came and went, of course, but I thought I'd give it a shot. "Can I treat you to dinner at a Greek restaurant?"

"The one on Broadway?"

I nodded.

"Companion Inventory is officially adjourned."

We caught light rail to Capitol Hill, practicing a bit of the limited sign language we'd studied together along the way. We really needed to resurrect School Night.

Heading for the escalator, I found it impossible not to remember the restaurant chef who'd been murdered on the platform a few months earlier, stabbed to death by a man experiencing a mental health crisis. But Tommy and I mostly focused on having a pleasant stroll up on Broadway. We passed Julia's, its front window filled with posters advertising their prestigious drag performers, and Lifelong thrift store, where I sometimes bought the T-shirts I donated to the archives. I enjoyed seeing the traffic signal boxes near the curb, painted with local LGBTQ heroes. On every block, on both sides of the street, a variety of Pride banners hung from light posts. A Rainbow flag, a Leather Pride flag, a Polyamory flag, a Trans flag, a Progressive Pride flag, and so on.

What would this street look like six months from now, I wondered?

Gay men our age would probably never feel completely safe, after everything we'd seen in our youth, the deliberate disregard for our lives during the height of the AIDS epidemic, the jokes made about our suffering.

Homosexuality had been classified as a mental illness until I was thirteen.

I couldn't tell if my worries now were a residual effect of those years, like folks who grew up during the Great Depression never being able to relax despite their economic comfort later.

How could I *not* push to find who had killed Salvador?

"Look!" Tommy stopped and pointed to a shuttered building across the street. It had originally been a movie theater, then later a drugstore for a local chain, and had been boarded up the past couple of years as the area fell into greater decay.

Someone had spray painted the words, "Deny Defend Depose!" on the wall. The words written by the man who'd assassinated a health insurance CEO a week or so earlier. People were already posting stickers with the slogan on lamp posts and bus stops. I'd seen several "Free Luigi" stickers, too.

The new president's buddies were already talking openly about privatizing Medicare and eliminating Medicaid.

Tommy pointed to a section of the wall beside the "Deny Defend Depose!" slogan. Several posters advertising a local production of "A Christmas Carol" covered the space.

As we continued our stroll, I had to control myself and not pull off a mini-poster advertising a live, interactive event for Dungeons and Drag Queens. It was right there on the light pole, just begging to be collected for a future mailing. But we were out to have a good time.

And we did. The Greek restaurant was lovely, the music low enough we could hear each other speak, and we talked only of pleasant things for the next hour. Tommy proposed that Alaskan cruise so we could finally admire the glaciers, and I suggested a few days in the Olympic National Forest. I'd turned a homemade quilt featuring bearded men and the traditional bear paw blocks into a sleeping bag. Tommy and I committed to stop postponing fun until "later."

There was a bit more tension at this point. I, at least, felt it, since a decent sex life had to be part of "fun."

It would be so easy not to say anything. We'd already had our Companion Inventory. Another difficult conversation could wait. I thought I'd overcome the temptation, but once we arrived back at the house, I couldn't stop myself any longer.

"Can I ask you a favor?" I took Tommy's hand.

"You can always *ask*."

"I know you don't want to have sex with me for now," I began, "but could you beat off onto my underwear? Please?"

Tommy twisted his mouth in thought for a moment before holding out his other hand. I pulled off my jeans, then pulled off my green boxer briefs and passed them over. Tommy headed for the bathroom and returned five minutes later.

"Here you go," he said. "Feel better?"

I held the underwear to my nose, inhaled, and then pulled them back on. "I do now," I said.

"I guess I need to court you again, too."

I smiled and gave him a peck. Greek food and sticky underwear were our love languages. We weren't fluent, but we committed again to practicing them more often.

Chapter Seven

First Hill Park was a small green space taking up perhaps half a city block on University Street not far from a leather bar on Pike. It featured a few trees, some occasionally mown grass, and a couple of benches. Not much else. The park was surrounded by tall apartment buildings and a lone First Hill mansion that survived changing times, converted now into an office. Spaces like this were scattered all across the city, Seattle parks making up almost 12% of the square footage of the city.

Detective Altan hadn't arrived yet, so I chose the one bench not occupied by homeless folks and waited. The drizzle had stopped hours ago, but the wood was still damp. Soiled food wrappers lay a few feet away, a determined crow struggling to extract its last calories.

When I looked up, the detective was almost upon me. He must have been waiting somewhere unseen. I started to stand but he waved me down, plopping onto the bench next to me. Rather than offer his hand in greeting, he placed it on my thigh.

"Good to see you, Bruce. Thanks for calling."

I didn't quite know what to do with his hand. I patted it once and then put both of mine in my lap.

"No need to cover up," Detective Altan said. "I've seen you in all your glory already."

"Uh…"

"Call me Demir."

What was going on? I knew our Sunday afternoon chat would be an off the record conversation—could you even have such a thing if neither of you was a reporter?—but I hadn't expected…was this flirtation?

I'd had another terrible nightmare last night, waking up screaming, and Tommy had insisted I contact Detective Altan first thing and get the counseling referral he'd offered. The detective had provided it over the phone but then suggested we meet in person today.

I took a breath now, staring at his nine o'clock shadow goatee, and told him the few bits of information I'd learned from Chris and Clayton over the past couple of days. Demir gently tilted my head so that I looked into his eyes, then took my right hand and held it with both of his.

"Interesting about Stu," he said. "And about Greg, too. We didn't know that. We did learn some problematic information about a few of the other men at JOB that night. Nothing I can share, I'm afraid." Demir lifted my hand to his lips and kissed it.

"Um…is this kosher?" I indicated my hand and his lips. Oops. "I mean, is this halal?" Damn. That was probably inappropriate, too.

Demir laughed. "You have a huge online presence," he said. "Saw photos of you on the Boeing picket line. Saw your movie review on a community blog about the neo-Nazis out on Whidbey Island. Even saw a photo of one of your quilts." He reached over and tweaked a nipple.

I only posted photos of my non-pornographic quilts, but I'd made a few of those as well. How wrong was I to wonder if I'd ever see him lying naked on top of one of them?

"Thanks, by the way, for showing up to so many pro-Palestine rallies."

Why did realizing Demir could easily learn what weren't even secrets still feel a bit creepy?

"And I know one of your favorite things to do in bed."

"Excuse me?"

"Research required me to read your profiles on a couple of hook up sites." He leaned over and whispered something fairly accurate in my ear. Then he turned my face to his and kissed me.

I kissed him back, feeling disoriented. He tasted good. Clean but not minty. And the man wasn't the slightest bit tongue-tied. His tongue reached deep into my mouth. I was technically versatile, but when it came to kissing, I much preferred another man's tongue filling my mouth than I did sliding my tongue into his. Most guys could only slip in an inch of tongue. When a man could fill my mouth with two or three inches, it kicked off a huge oxytocin release in my brain.

What the hell were we doing?

When Demir pulled away, he leaned back on the bench, still holding my hand. My head was reeling a bit from the unexpected intimacy, and I'll use that as an excuse for why I blurted out my next question.

"How did the murderer keep from getting sprayed with blood when he slit Salvador's throat?"

"Mr. Castro was already dead."

"How did he manage not to track footprints in all that blood?"

Demir shrugged. "He must have stepped away quickly." He looked into my eyes. His were golden brown. Demir surveyed the rest of my face, stopping at my ears. He leaned over and stuck his tongue into the nearest one. Then he turned my face toward him and kissed me on the lips again.

I liked sex a lot. But I liked kissing just as much. Lots of guys weren't into kissing at all, so it was hard now to pull myself away, even if I knew all of this was inappropriate.

I say "hard to pull myself away" because I think I *could* have done it. I simply chose not to.

"No secondary DNA that we can talk about." Demir's fingers caressed the back of my neck. I must have frowned without realizing it because he added, "I'm off duty. I can kiss whoever I want on my own time."

"Are you sure your personal ethics correspond to your department's guidelines?"

He laughed. "You'd be surprised what our guidelines allow."

I decided not to pursue that. After all, it could mean pretty much anything. And that information seemed to be on a "need *not* to know" basis, unless I wanted my dreams to feel even more troubled.

"Do *your* guidelines include telling your husband you kissed the detective on the case?"

"They don't require it," I said. "I just do it anyway. He's not required to tell me if he plays, either, but I like when he does because I like knowing he's having a good time." I pulled out my phone and showed Demir a photo of Tommy.

"He looks Persian."

Tommy could pass for Latino, Arabic, Persian, or indigenous. He could pass for white in the right light. Or mixed. It was one of the things that first attracted me to him, an indeterminant everyman with something about his looks not quite "standard," something you couldn't quite put your finger on. Then when I'd heard him say "Duwamish," everything clicked into place.

A short, black woman wearing several layers of clothing paused at an overflowing trash can a few feet away. "F!" she shouted. "C! S! M! A! O! L! C!" She picked up a piece of trash from the ground, tried to put it in the trash can, and watched it fall to the ground again. "D! A! L! Q! M! I!"

"Let's take a walk," Demir suggested.

"Where to?"

"Freeway Park?"

Demir had suggested a park built partially over the freeway cutting through downtown. Did he know how seedy it had grown in recent years?

He was a detective. Of course he knew.

We chatted along the short walk there. Demir knew about my Mormon past. He told me now about his parents moving to the U.S. before he was born and about visiting family still in Turkey. "The country managed to stay secular for almost a century," he said, "but it's controlled more by its religious right all the time, too."

I was unfortunately already aware, just from the little Turkish television I watched. "When the investigation is over, would you like to come to the house sometime and watch *Midnight at the Pera Palace* with me?"

"Are you asking me on a date, Bruce?" Demir's eyes twinkled.

"Is it a date if dinner's not included? If it's just a blow job and a movie?"

"I'll look it up in the guidelines."

Finally in the park, we found an unoccupied bench and began kissing again. I watched out of the corner of my eye as a homeless man missing a shoe staggered by. His skin was that shade of red which indicated infection rather than cold, though it was probably in the mid-forties.

"So if there was no secondary DNA on the underwear in Salvador's mouth," I said, "it must have been his own." Technically, he'd only said there was no secondary DNA he could "talk about."

Demir shrugged. "Or a new pair bought especially to use as a weapon that night." He pulled my chin down to open my mouth and thrust his tongue back in.

A minute or so later, I asked the obvious follow up. "Premeditated?"

Demir shrugged and kissed me again. I could get used to this. It had been years since Tommy and I did more than peck.

"Why me?" I asked, pulling back. "I know I found the body, but I don't know any more than anyone else there. Why are you talking to *me*?" In person. With tongue. He could easily have insisted on a phone call. Or any other type of normal interaction.

Demir held my hand with both of his and put it in his lap. I managed not to make the joke he must have heard a hundred times about being happy to see someone. "How many men," he asked, "do you think would feel comfortable kissing while talking about a brutal murder?"

He liked me because I was weird? Hmm. That was…um…*weird.*

"I watched you handle one of the most awful experiences of your life way better than most." He gave me a wry smile. "As a homicide detective, I can tell you that anyone I have a relationship with, whether that's my parents or a boyfriend or any friend at all, usually gets uncomfortable at some point with how often I switch from casual conversation to gruesome details."

I remembered years ago dating an ER nurse and our conversations over dinner.

"I've been deliberately switching back and forth today to see…"

"If we have a future?" I grinned, hopefully not dismissively.

Demir grinned back. "You're handling it like a champion," he said.

I wasn't sure that was something to be proud of. I could remember many times at work or social events when I'd be chatting with someone and bring up a topic too taboo for that environment. Nothing horrible. Maybe colonoscopies or toenail fungus. Or composting a human body rather than having a traditional burial. There was a certain look people got in their eyes right before they found an excuse to walk away from you.

"An Olympic champion," Demir continued, "from 2500 years ago, back when they competed without clothes."

"Have you considered making some extra money writing greeting cards?"

"How do you know I don't?"

I pulled him close and kissed him again. We chatted a while longer, about Tommy, about the bar in White Center where Demir liked to play darts, about the dangers inherent in hooking up with strangers in bathhouses, online, or at jack off clubs.

About how even among the marginalized, both of us were outliers. While a certain segment of gay subculture might like uniforms, LGBTQ folks as a whole weren't big fans of the police.

"But I never did have sex in a park or bathroom," I said. And I knew a lot of guys who'd done that. I suppose we all had our limits.

"Good," he said. "Because that kind of thing is dangerous on several levels. I'll email you a few links to self-defense videos," he said. "In case there's any trouble next time you're at JOB."

We hugged goodbye. And that was that. Had we just gone on a date? Was this a semi-professional chat? Might we someday actually be friends?

Whatever the case, I'd enjoyed it and couldn't wait to talk to Tommy. First, though, I headed back up to Capitol Hill to join the practice picket line in front of the coffeeshop for an hour.

And didn't think about sex, murder, or toenail fungus.

I thought about living wages and a decent work/life balance.

In the breakroom at the courthouse a few days earlier, someone had put a small whiteboard on the wall, posing the question, "What do you want for Christmas?"

Some of my coworkers had responded with comments like, "A million dollars," "A new car," "Season tickets to the Seahawks," and "A trip around the world."

I'd waited until no one else was in the room and written, "World peace."

Yeah, I knew it was corny. But I meant it. Even if I was nowhere near as congenial as Sandra Bullock.

Humans were a terribly flawed species. And possibly on our way out. But in the meantime, I wanted to hope. So I chose to do so.

Chapter Eight

Life seemed to get back to normal on Monday. A regular day at work with no especially awful interactions. On my commute home, I received a text from Demir with a photo of his front porch. I sent him a selfie back of me on the bus.

After dinner, Tommy and I sat on the sofa holding hands while we watched TV. Lots of couples established a Date Night to keep things interesting. We'd had to establish a Homebody Night to counteract all our other activities.

After we finished another episode of *Inspector Ricciardi*, Tommy and I headed off to our separate offices. He played online Solitaire tonight while I watched videos on how to break someone's fingers, how to gouge someone's eyes, and how to crush someone's balls.

Yikes.

Tuesday after work, I met my friend Nathan in Columbia City. We'd first met over a year earlier at a Gaza rally. He was Jewish, about seventy, a bit short, with a thick moustache that felt good against my lips or other body parts. He wasn't "good looking for his age" but outright hot. I'd have been attracted to him even when I was thirty. I rarely felt I was "settling" when I had sex with an older man, and definitely not with Nathan.

I felt the same with Tommy. Once, while we'd been looking through old photos, I'd pointed to an especially alluring one from a trip we'd taken on our fifth anniversary. "Too bad I don't look like that anymore," Tommy had said.

"That's who I see every time I look at you," I'd responded in all honesty. It was as if I could see him in multiple iterations simultaneously as he changed over the years. And because he looked good in almost every version, the amalgamation in my head was an overall image of beauty.

"Want to split a sandwich?" Nathan asked. Since Wednesday was my day off, I could stay up a little later the evening before. Sometimes, Nathan and I ate dinner together. Other times, we saw a movie. On still other occasions, I headed straight to his place after work and we'd cuddle for a couple of hours on his sofa.

The first time Tommy had walked in on us at our place, Nathan had felt awkward, but he soon learned we both meant it when we said we supported each other's friendships.

Nathan and I popped inside a sandwich and chips shop on Rainier Avenue, finding a table away from the window. He felt the cold easily and preferred sitting closer to the kitchen. We talked about a movie he'd seen over the weekend with another friend and about the latest political news.

"I think the first person just died of bird flu in the U.S.," I said. "And North Korean troops are now fighting for Russia in Ukraine."

Nathan sighed. "My nephew's married to a Christian," he said. "She's nice enough, but…"

"They think you're going to hell?" I asked.

"They sent me a Christmas card showing their two children standing in front of an American flag and a bald eagle." He scrunched his nose.

"Nothing says Peace on Earth like a bird of prey."

"I hate all this conflating of religion and politics."

"They want Armageddon," I said, "so they can force Jesus to return." God was all powerful, but apparently not so powerful he couldn't be manipulated by his imperfect human subjects.

After my excommunication, I'd wished for a while to be able to go back to believing. Then I'd wished God was real so people who did cruel things in his name could face eternal consequences. Now I just hoped good people stood up for each other even when it was scary to do so.

Nathan had received a low lottery number during the last years of the Vietnam war and applied for Conscientious Objector status. His opposition to war began long before the latest escalation of the Nakba. Given the incoming administration, Christian nationalists were likely to get what they wanted in the Middle East.

"Sometimes, I'm glad I'm old." Nathan had experienced a mild heart attack several months before I met him.

"I'm not afraid of dying," I said. "I just don't want to give fascists the satisfaction of being the ones to kill me."

During some low periods, I'd even hoped to be diagnosed with terminal cancer.

Nathan put his hands over his ears but smiled as he did so. "I'm going to need dessert after all this gloomy talk." I reached across the table and squeezed his hand.

"My friend Chris from the Jack Off club told me one of the regulars there signs up his single friends for life insurance, making himself the beneficiary." He'd texted me today at work, asking me to call him, and during my break, he told me what he'd learned about Andrew, Salvador's ex. Chris said Detective Downey assured him they were already aware.

"That's kind of creepy."

"The guy pays the premiums himself."

Nathan shuddered, and I squeezed his hand again.

"I talked to Tommy," I said. "He's obviously my first beneficiary on my bank accounts, but I've amended my will so that if he precedes me, you're next in line."

"Oh, uh…"

"The house is in my name only. It goes to Tommy when I die, but if he precedes me, it goes to one of his nieces." My very tiny effort at reparations, since the U.S. government was never going to address it.

We talked a few more minutes about awkward end-of-life matters. I hadn't even learned of the death of a favorite aunt until almost a year after the fact because no one in the family had wanted to talk to me. I'd found out accidentally through a friend of a friend on Facebook.

Finally, it was time for tiramisu. We split a piece and I fed Nathan over the table, deliberately smudging a little on his lower lip so I could lean over and lick it off.

"My friend Chris also told me that Salvador recently returned from a trip to Mexico. Flew down from Seattle and came back the very next day."

"A mule?"

I shrugged. "I overheard Sal boasting a few events ago that he could take the biggest dick available up his ass…" So theoretically, lots of room for contraband in there. "I didn't see anyone at the party take him up on the offer." It would have just been an exchange of phone numbers, obviously. I practiced memorizing seven digits before each event, since I couldn't very well walk around the playroom with a pen and paper.

Though I suppose with a large enough nipple ring and a magnetized clip to hold a notepad…

"I need to meet this Chris someday," Nathan said. We'd committed early on to introduce each other to whatever friends we knew, to help counteract the Seattle Freeze. "Meet another person in real life."

"I finally got off Facebook." I'd found myself wasting far too much time, almost always coming away unhappy, rarely thinking, "Boy, it's great staying connected with folks." I'd miss the Moss Appreciation Society and Queer

Quilters and the gay artists I followed, but those weren't the posts taking up 90% of my time on the site.

"I don't know if I could do that."

"I don't think everyone needs to," I said.

"How will you stay in touch with people?"

"Email. Phone."

He gasped.

"I know." Young people almost never emailed, if I could judge by my coworkers. They didn't knock or ring doorbells anymore, either, just texted their friends, "I'm here," and waited for the door to open.

Old people had our own language, words no longer in use, allusions younger folks didn't understand. It was almost like a secret code, the way "kids these days" couldn't read cursive. I'd heard so much about older people being digital immigrants because computers and smart phones and other tech would just never feel natural to us. But all of this made us social immigrants as well, even in the gay community, where we no longer fit. Younger gays looked at us as if we were speaking another language.

Because we were.

Nathan and I talked about the murder at the jack off club as we continued eating. I recounted everything I'd learned from the various players about the possible suspects. Going over it all again didn't reveal some obvious point I'd missed.

But on our walk over to the movie theater two blocks away, Nathan did ask a question I hadn't considered.

"Do you know if he owned property someone else wanted to develop? There are lots of apartment buildings going up all over Seattle lately."

I could imagine Salvador being a hold out and getting on a buyer's nerves. And murder to gain access to property was part of the plot of *The Turkish Bath*, the first movie I'd seen Mehmet Gunsür in.

"The next event's this Saturday," I said. "I want to hide behind the New Member Orientation curtain and listen to people in the locker room. I want to hide in a bathroom stall and eavesdrop. But obviously, no one's going to be openly talking about the man they just killed."

"If there's no progress on the case," Nathan said, "the detectives might have to move on to something else."

"Maybe I'll drop hints that I heard the detectives are just about to make an arrest and *then* hide and eavesdrop."

"So you'll either be killed next or charged with interfering in an investigation."

He had a point. The case had always been out of my hands, but it was clear that whatever motivation I had for keeping my nose in it wasn't going to be enough. I felt so much freer now after deleting my FB account that I wanted to focus on that freedom. If that was more time for sex, great. If it just meant staying home and reading a book on the porch, that was fine, too. I'd recently purchased *Dying of Curiosity*, and it looked promising.

In the lobby of the tiny theater a couple of blocks away, I thought I saw Stu from JOB look my way before darting into the bathroom.

JOB had a Fight Club rule. If we ran into anyone from the club in another setting, we weren't supposed to acknowledge them. Maybe they'd have no problem with it, but perhaps they wouldn't want to answer awkward questions from whoever they might be with. Like, "Where do you know that guy from?"

On our second date, Tommy and I had run into a guy on Broadway he seemed to know well. "Hey, Tommy," the man said, giving him a hug. "I haven't seen you since the orgy at the bathhouse." I'd wanted to feign shock and horror but couldn't keep myself from laughing.

Nathan and I bought our tickets and made our way to the middle of the second largest theater. Given his height, Nathan needed an unobstructed view of the screen. I put my arm around his shoulders, and we relaxed as the lights dimmed.

Not that Hugh Grant in *Heretic* promised a serene evening. The two women playing the missionaries were both ex-Mormon. Nathan put his hand on my thigh, and I squeezed his shoulder. Even after all these years as an out gay man, I never tired of casual physical touch. It always struck me as miraculous, a divine gift, if I'd believed in the Divine.

Watching the story unfold, it was impossible not to reflect at least briefly on my own missionary days. The times teenage boys had spit on us, or kicked us, or thrown fist-sized rocks at us. The time someone chased us down a deserted, muddy road in their car, passing us again and again, spraying mud on us with each pass.

The time my companion threatened to break my fingers.

The time another companion took a dump in the bushes at Capodimonte because he couldn't wait until we made it back home.

The time one of my district leaders had a nervous breakdown and had to be sent back to the U.S. for his health.

Two missionaries in Tommy's mission had even been kidnapped and held for ransom. The LDS church never paid in those situations, but the police eventually rescued the young men three weeks later.

I looked at Hugh Grant's smiling face up on the screen and remembered one of the first lessons we'd learned in religious salesmanship. "Look for people who've had a recent job loss," our mission president told us. "Or who moved to a new city. Anyone who's had a serious illness or lost a child." I remembered the earnest smile on the president's face. "These are folks who will now be ready to hear the gospel."

Teaching nineteen-year-old kids how to emotionally manipulate and abuse others, a skill many Mormons continued to hone the rest of their lives.

It struck me that questioning guys from the jack off club while we were having sex wasn't all that different. Taking advantage of them when their defenses were down to see if they'd let something slip.

Was Demir flirting with me to keep me from realizing he was still investigating me?

Just as the two young women in the movie realize they're trapped in the psychopath's house, a loud whooping noise began blaring throughout the theater and the lights began to flash.

"Active shooter," an automated voice called out. "Please evacuate."

Nathan's fingers dug into my leg.

"Active shooter," the message repeated between whoops. "Please evacuate."

People in the room began scrambling. Nathan jumped up and I followed. No one was screaming, other than a few frantic Oh gods and God damns. A couple of Shits and Fucks.

We followed a small group of young adults out a back exit into the alley behind the theater and kept running, our breath sending out staccato puffs of fog every few seconds like gunshot smoke. The clattering of feet against the pavement made me remember the scene from *The Birds* where the children flee the school. I didn't hear any shots and figured the shooter must have been in the other small theater beside ours.

Was that really Stu I'd seen earlier? And was he after *me*?

A block away, Nathan grabbed onto a signpost and leaned over, breathing heavily, fog dissipating almost as soon as it formed.

"You okay?"

He nodded but couldn't speak yet. He sometimes had asthma attacks in the winter.

I turned back to make sure no one with a gun had followed us. A last couple of stragglers were still exiting the building.

No gunshots.

"Whew!" Nathan managed a moment later. "Just out of breath." He inhaled deeply a couple more times but didn't reach for the emergency inhaler I knew he carried with him.

I was still breathing heavily myself but about to suggest we start moving again when we heard someone calling from the rear exit of the theater. "False alarm!" The man wore a Polo shirt with the theater's name on the front. I'd seen him at the refreshment counter when we'd first walked in.

"False alarm!" he shouted again. "We'll give everyone a free pass for another showing!"

Nathan choked out a laugh. "I think I'll pass on the free pass."

I nodded. "Let's get you home."

As we slowly walked the five blocks to Nathan's place, I wondered if we'd learn any more details on the news. Had someone deliberately tripped that alarm? A disgruntled employee?

Stu?

I didn't even realize Active Shooter alarms were a thing.

I could imagine Sal's killer trying to disguise a second murder by making it part of a mass shooting. But why would Stu, even if he *was* the murderer, want to come after me? I didn't know anything.

What was the saying? "Even paranoids have enemies." I could imagine a few people who knew me and some who didn't who might like me dead.

That probably included Tommy on some days.

Ever since COVID shut things down in the state back in March of 2020, I'd felt a heightened sense of mortality. What if, for one reason or another, my time was up in a few weeks? Or a few days?

I leaned over to inhale Nathan's scent.

Once we reached his place, I asked to come inside and use the bathroom. I felt an urgent need to pee. Again. We hugged goodbye, kissed, I breathed in his scent one last time, and then I headed out to the bus stop and home to my husband.

Chapter Nine

Tommy and I didn't see eye to eye on things like "danger." He didn't consciously try to one up me, but if I mentioned worries about unjust arrests under fascism, he'd point out that Leonard Peltier was still in prison. If I mentioned RFK, Jr. undermining vaccines, he'd bring up blankets infected with smallpox. If I questioned what the new president might say if told by the Supreme Court he couldn't do something and wanted to do it anyway, he'd quote Andrew Jackson.

Nothing new under the sun, I supposed.

Even I didn't feel especially traumatized by the false alarm yesterday. It was both impressive and depressing how quickly humans adapted. Some survivors of actual mass shootings had survived more than one.

But we all had areas where we refused to adapt at all. "We don't need any more pasta sauce," Tommy told me when I came home with two bags of groceries from an outlet chain Wednesday morning.

"They were forty-nine cents each," I said.

"We have enough sauce to get through the apocalypse," he insisted.

Because of our Mormon background, raised with the commandment to store at least a year's supply of food for emergencies (a two-year supply was better), Tommy hated when I bought food on sale. My view was that it might be six more months before pasta sauce was that cheap again, if ever, and it wasn't as if it was going to spoil. Neither did canned green beans when they were fifty cents a can or when a forty-ounce box of wheat crackers cost ninety-eight cents.

A forty-two ounce jar of sugar-free peanut butter for $4.98 could last twenty years. Why not buy eight jars when I had the chance?

What if the new administration made firing people for being gay legal again? What if it became mandatory?

"We have a whole pantry full of food," Tommy said. "Where are you going to put all that peanut butter?"

"I have room under my side of the bed."

He slapped his head and walked away.

Was that for, "Oops, I could have had a year's supply"?

Honestly, though, Tommy seemed to have a distorted view of how long a pantry full of food could last if no new food was added to it. If we weren't rationing, a single can of green beans was hardly enough to function as a meal for two people. If we needed the equivalent of two cans of food per meal and ate just two meals a day, that would require at least a hundred and twenty cans of food per month.

Even a jar of peanut butter, if you weren't spreading it on a piece of bread to make it last longer, would empty pretty quickly. All the food we had in every cabinet in the kitchen would probably not last more than two or three months.

And I wanted enough to help our neighbors, too. We could hardly eat happily knowing they were starving next door. Most people, after all, had far less on hand than we did.

I'd grown up with a separate freezer the same size as a refrigerator. But Tommy and I had just the one routine appliance, with only a fraction set aside for frozen goods. Just how many packs of frozen veggie patties could one fit in such a space? We had five of them, plus six packs of various frozen vegetables, a few frozen loaves of keto bread, and not much else.

If things got bad enough that we needed two years of food storage, I didn't actually want to stick around for two years. But I did want enough on hand that I could better plan my own exit from this world if the situation required it. Just before the pandemic, I'd bought a handgun without telling Tommy. I'd never used it, not even at a shooting range, but needed to know I *could* leave if necessary. Right-wing moralists were trying to deny terminally ill patients Death with Dignity meds all the time.

I didn't suppose having a gun hidden in my office gave me *much* peace of mind, but it did give me *some*.

Like most couples, on many topics, Tommy and I were in near-perfect agreement. On others, while we might be adjacent books on a shelf, we definitely weren't on the same page.

Since it was as important to keep the peace now as it was to eat later, I agreed not to buy any more pasta sauce.

I didn't make any promises about peanut butter, though. And I ordered another box of high fiber penne online.

After putting everything away, I headed back out to meet with the counselor Demir had suggested. Rain had begun to fall when I stepped off the bus in Mount Baker. The therapist's office was only a block from the Lighthouse for the Blind, so I was still mostly dry when I arrived.

Dr. Nethery wasn't a doctor, but I felt too uncomfortable calling her Ms. Nethery and kept calling her Doctor, anyway, making her uncomfortable instead. We discussed my nightmares, whether I felt emotionally safe around Tommy despite our lack of physical intimacy, and even my compulsion to investigate from the sidelines. Then she asked if I'd considered meeting with a sex therapist until I felt safe returning to a group sex setting.

"I'm not sure the county health insurance plan covers that," I said.

"Do you think Tommy would agree to a temporary lift of the marital sex ban until the murder is solved?"

"Oh, I wouldn't want to ask. He might feel obligated but hate every second of it."

She nodded. "And could you agree to a temporary suspension of sex with strangers? Even for a couple of weeks?"

When she said it like that, I felt stupid for not considering it sooner. When Tommy and I had spoken about it, the suspension had felt indefinite. I could easily agree to two weeks and then reassess after.

"Yes," I said. "I can do that." I was already scheduled for the clean-up shift this Saturday, but I could show up at the end of check-in, remain in the lobby and never undress or be alone with anyone in the bathroom or locker room. That should keep me safe while also helping me feel I wasn't missing out totally.

We wrapped up the meeting a few minutes later. I made a return appointment for the following Thursday. I might need a few more visits, but I was pretty sure my insurance only covered six sessions, as if there was *any* issue serious enough to require a therapist that could be resolved so quickly.

On my way home from today's session, I caught the 106 heading south and ended up with another mental health boost. Bus drivers almost always either ignored me as I boarded or gave me a scowl. It was impossible to know if they were just continually stressed from interacting with the public or if they were reacting to my white maleness or the general state of the world. But today, the Latino driver greeted me warmly.

I smiled back. Since I always wore my mask on public transit, I hoped he could at least see the smile in my eyes.

Somewhere along MLK, the driver stopped and two homeless men boarded, both white. One of the men was probably around forty while the other looked to be several years older, hard to tell given the hard lives they lived. One of the men walked straight to the back of the bus, muttering to himself the way folks with mental illness sometimes do. The other man pushed a baby carriage filled with personal belongings on board. Someone across the aisle from me groaned.

Strollers, shopping carts, wheelchairs, and anything else of the sort could stop a bus for five minutes if the person boarding didn't know how to navigate. "Thank you, Driver," the man with the baby stroller said. "We're only going down one stop, to the 7-11. I'll get this hooked up in five seconds and we're good to go."

I could see the driver nod to the homeless man. "Better than walking in the rain," he said pleasantly.

I tried to remember that while a wannabe dictator had won the election last month, those voters only represented something like 27% of the population. A lot, to be sure, but not the majority they pretended to be.

Two stops later, the man with the baby carriage called out to the man in back, "We're here." He was taking care of the mentally ill man, I realized, making sure he got where he needed to go. He could have teamed up with anyone else on the street but chose to associate with this guy. As the man with the carriage moved to exit through the front, an Asian woman sitting in the Disability section handed him some money. He thanked her, thanked the driver, and the two men stepped off the bus.

An all too rare display of humanity. Maybe, I thought, we'd get through these next few years, after all.

Chris was due to return for another playdate on Friday evening, so I texted him mid-afternoon to check that plans were still on. Established sex buddies weren't included in the temporary sex suspension, were they? Instead of sending a thumbs up emoji or something similar, he called. "I'm on my work break," he said, "getting hard thinking about Friday."

Guys said things like this all the time, even while they were eating cereal or taking out the trash. It was supposed to be sexy talk. It did little for me, but I usually tried to play along. I made a couple of lackluster quips back and then told him about the false alarm at the theater and my suspicion I may have seen Stu in the building.

"Interesting," he said. "I've been using some of the guys from JOB as homework assignments for my PI class. So I know Stu did purchase a gun recently."

"But no one was actually shooting yesterday."

"He also signed up for some self-defense courses."

"Given the political climate," I said, "we should probably *all* do that." I remembered the short video I'd watched that morning before leaving the house.

Chris laughed. "True, but it means he could have used some of the moves he learned to overcome Salvador."

I frowned. How in the world did detectives piece together all the suspicious information about suspects to form an answer? Suspicions, after all, were nothing more than that. I wanted to ask Chris something specific to research about Stu but had no idea what to ask.

"Any way you can check his bank statements?" I asked.

Chris guffawed so loudly he almost choked. "Not a chance."

And what would that have proven anyway? Perhaps I could ask Stu if Chris and I could come over for a threeway, and while Stu and I were engaged, Chris might do a bit of snooping. But that scenario quickly felt way too creepy.

"My professor says that investigating means understanding how magicians work. 'Look at *this* hand instead of *that* hand.'"

"What if the murderer has both hands behind his back?"

Chris laughed.

"Well," I said, "thanks for the information. Can't wait to see you on Friday."

"Me, too." He chuckled. "I've got some fun plans."

After we hung up, I took my own advice and watched a few more YouTube videos on self-defense. How to break a nose, how to break a knee, even how to break a neck. Oh dear. Of course, watching a video wasn't the same thing as practicing the actual moves. No way to get muscle memory without using muscles. I stood away from my desk and tried to go through the motions, but alone, without a training partner, it wasn't much.

And it felt embarrassing to ask Tommy or another friend to train with me. I'd look like an idiot. Or we might actually break each other's nose.

I did a load of laundry, read more of *Dying of Curiosity*, and scrolled a few more minutes on YouTube, looking for news. A ski resort in Turkey had burned, killing at least seventy-nine people. Horrific.

I texted Demir to offer my condolences.

Then I turned on Pandora and listened to music while I took a nap.

Tommy and I watched a Belgian comedy/mystery show called *Chantal* during dinner, and then we settled down to another game of Scrabble. I went first and used a J for the opening double score word. E-J-E-C-T.

Tommy added a D to the front of the word and then kept writing in a different direction, completing the word D-E-C-R-Y.

"Should we bet on the final score?" I asked with a smile.

"Not yet. Let me get further ahead first."

I stuck out my tongue. He looked for a moment as if he might lean over and suck it into his mouth.

But he didn't.

Chapter Ten

At the courthouse on Thursday, I saw that one of the trials was for a man accused of beating a homeless woman to death with a baseball bat while she slept on the sidewalk. He was claiming self-defense, apparently, insisting that her presence near his store kept customers away. He was losing money, would soon lose his business and then his home. He had no choice.

As a kid, I'd wanted to read comic books starring the Three Nephites. Everyone knew there was no such thing as Spiderman or Captain America. The Three Nephites were real and went around helping people all the time. They'd even stepped up once to stop a man from breaking into our home.

It wasn't until years later I realized my parents had staged the whole thing, to help instill "faith" in us kids.

There were no Nephites to help that poor homeless woman. *We* had to be the superheroes.

I tried to tell that story to a coworker during lunch, but he wasn't interested. I saw the look in his eyes just before he glanced at his watch. I'd become the boring old man who kept telling stories of his youth.

"It's okay, Marcus," I said. "I spent most of my life not having any relevant anecdotes to tell. By the time I finally do, no one wants to hear them."

"Oh, it's not that!" Marcus sputtered.

I smiled. "I did the same thing when I was young. We didn't want to listen to old guys rambling about their lives, either."

"Oh, but…"

"It's okay."

I had time to watch one self-defense video before returning to my station. How to get out of a chokehold.

After the new administration took office in January, I wondered what kinds of stories and anecdotes young people would soon amass in their repertoire. Stories that would probably be ignored the next time fascism rose up, the way we were ignoring the stories of the handful of Holocaust survivors still around today.

During dinner that evening, Tommy and I listened to a podcast on Radiolab about a triad of bald eagles, two males and a female who set up a nest together to raise their young. When the female was killed in an attack, the two males finished raising their young together and the following year introduced another female to the nest, creating another triad.

Just before bedtime, I heard Tommy in the bathroom beating off. He tried to be quiet but made an unmistakable hiss when he came.

I slept fitfully but didn't hear the attack sometime in the middle of the night. When I opened the door to leave for work in the morning, I saw that someone had thrown three eggs against the front of the house.

A teen prank? Someone from the club? A neighbor upset with white people? Perhaps someone who didn't like Native Americans?

It could have even been another Native American. The Duwamish weren't recognized federally or by several other local tribal nations, who actively opposed granting them recognition. It was complicated, much of the grief due to U.S. policies and treaties, but I'd also learned ages ago that tribal membership wasn't determined *at all* by DNA.

I remembered that Nazis had killed a Catholic nun because her ancestry was Jewish.

I also remembered that when I'd come out years ago, I'd written letters to the editor about gay rights, had announced it in a talk at church. I wanted to make sure I'd be on someone's list, so that if things ever got bad, I'd know I couldn't pass but would need to fight.

I was likely on several lists.

"I'll clean it up," Tommy told me. "You'll be late for work."

We kissed, and I headed off to the bus stop.

The rest of the day felt dreary, and not only because of the steady drizzle. I was spending every work hour surrounded by criminals. Some of the crimes were petty, others more serious. Was this really what I wanted to do until the day I died?

I supposed this was also a glass half full/half empty Rorschach test. I could instead see the courts as a place where innocent people (or, at the very least, those not guilty) were released and sent home after their trials.

I texted Chris during my lunch break to confirm he was coming over tonight while Tommy went to dinner with friends. I stopped at Safeway on the way home to pick up a slice of lemon poppyseed cake for Tommy and walked the rest of the way uphill to the house. Even when we spent most of the evening apart, we still tried to share a moment of connection. Since he'd cleaned up the eggs this morning, he deserved a treat.

"I've got fresh sheets ready for after you guys play," Tommy told me on his way out the door. It was time to change them, anyway.

Tommy was gone less than a minute when Chris texted he was here. "I'm still grungy from work," I said. "Want to jump in the shower with me?"

Chris laughed. "I'll chill out and listen to music to wind down from *my* day. And after you dry off, I'll see if I can't get you all dirty again."

It wasn't until I found Chris lying spread eagled in the bedroom fifteen minutes later that I noticed he'd brought supplies. His open bag lay on the floor, while beside him on the bed lay a double-headed dildo, nipple clamps, and some warming lube promising to gently burn whatever body part it touched.

I climbed on top, started kissing, and we got down to business.

Our afterglow session later felt more like afterburn, what with the new lube. But this time was still one of the best parts of sex—feeling close enough to another person to say things that so often went unsaid.

"In a perfect world," I began, "I'd live next door to my husband, not with him."

"Really?" Chris laughed.

"Or maybe down the block or around the corner. Close but not too close."

"Why's that?" Chris turned onto his side to look at me.

"Living together is the hardest part. The different ways we wash dishes or clean the house. The way he doesn't like my clutter but is fine with his, the fact that he likes it ten degrees hotter in the house than I do."

"Not the way you like it ten degrees colder than he does?"

I laughed now, too. "It's all about the perspective."

We chatted a bit more. It was difficult to share details of problems I was having with Tommy. It felt too much like a betrayal. But if I couldn't talk to friends to help me sort through things, was I condemned to figure everything out on my own? I supposed if I could make myself talk to Tommy about whatever issue we were having, that would be the best solution, but most of our problems existed because we both found it so difficult to talk. A Companion Inventory was great, but we couldn't have one every day, and we often struggled in the interim.

Chris listened without offering advice, which I appreciated. Of course, I *wanted* to hear "the solution," but that part really was up to Tommy and me.

Chris mentioned a couple of minor issues at his workplace, and then he turned to Jack Off Buddies. "I sucked Marin's dick last night. He said at the last event, he overheard Stu and Andrew arguing about Sal."

"What about?"

"Marin couldn't hear very well. The music gets loud in there."

"No details at all?"

Chris shrugged. "Something about money. Marin said he wasn't trying to listen. Only remembered it later."

"Pity."

"Marin did say that being big is almost like being invisible."

I'd often thought that neither Sean Connery nor Daniel Craig could have been spies in real life. Their looks alone made it impossible not to be noticed wherever they went.

"Do you ever think about killing some right-wing creep?" Chris asked out of the blue.

"Excuse me?"

"How would you get close enough to someone who mattered?" he went on, looking up at the ceiling. I noticed a cobweb I needed to brush away. "Not just an average bigot. Someone with influence or power. Someone whose absence would makes things noticeably better."

"Um…"

Chris chuckled. "I guess that murder at the club has me thinking. We were all right there, and this guy still got away. I can't help but wonder how people manage it."

To be honest, similar thoughts *had* crossed my mind, but these were some dark musings that even afterglow couldn't make space for in conversation. "No one I'd have access to is worth ruining my life over," I said. If I was afraid of fascists sending me to prison, volunteering outright for imprisonment was hardly the solution.

Chris nodded. "The Brutus would need to be someone in the inner circle of these jerks. But those aren't people likely to do anything." He sighed. "I guess we'll have to be content with bread and circuses."

"Stress eating in front of the TV?"

Chris chuckled. "Fucking and sucking."

"I can get behind that."

"And in front of it?"

"And under and over. A sandwich, made with *two* pieces of bread."

"Now that's a circus I'd like to join."

After Chris left, I put the fresh sheets on the bed, did a load of laundry, and got Tommy's coffee ready to go for Saturday morning.

I probably needed a less philosophical playmate. Chris might not be the best match for my own ruminating personality. Perhaps at tomorrow afternoon's event, I'd meet someone new.

Astonishing how my sex life had transformed from parched to almost lush in the space of a few months. The change had required hard work, without a question. But the most important factor had simply been making the decision in the first place.

I smiled, remembering a verse from the Book of Mormon promising that for those who had faith, "weak things" could "become strong unto them."

If I'd known the Book of Mormon could be so useful, I might have read it cover to cover more than the ten times I did.

Well, eleven, if you counted the time I read it in Italian.

Chapter Eleven

"I'm heading to the Jack Off Club." I gave Tommy a kiss, superficial, but kept my lips pressed to his longer than usual, more than our typical peck.

His brows furrowed. "I'll probably spend a couple of hours at the gym," he said. "Maybe I'll finally be up to joining you one of these days."

I opened our speakeasy door but turned back. "If you can wait," I began, "don't shower until you get home."

"We're not showering together," he stated firmly.

"I'd like to watch you, Tommy. I want to *see* you. I *like* looking at you."

He pressed his lips. "Hmm."

"I mean, I won't object if you're up for a bit of rimming after you dry off, but I won't insist."

He closed his eyes for a moment and nodded. "I did say I was going to court you again."

I pumped my fist. "Yay! Ass time when I get home!" And then maybe some Scrabble. "It Takes Two, Baby," I remembered Donny and Marie singing.

"You said you were just going to watch." He wagged a finger.

"Isn't it still watching if I do it an inch away from your asshole?"

Tommy walked toward me and pulled me into another kiss. Still tongueless, but at least a lingering kiss. "You have fun at the club, Bruce."

I smiled all the way to Capitol Hill, even when two police officers brought their bomb-sniffing dog on board light rail. Once on Broadway, I stepped around two homeless men, one wearing a ragged blanket, arguing in front of a bar that featured axe throwing contests. Half a block farther down, I pried a small poster off a light pole. "Queer Christmas Caroling at Cal Anderson."

Guilt and victory were odd feelings to experience simultaneously.

Soon I was at the club, waiting until exactly 1:00 before opening the door. No admittance even a minute early. I didn't want to hang out right in front, though, so I pretended to study some fliers on another light pole a few doors down. The air was cold and moist, but there was no drizzle. When I saw one of the regulars go inside a few minutes later, I walked the rest of the way over.

I always felt a bit nervous walking into Jack Off Buddies, despite attending on multiple occasions. Would it be *this time* that someone I knew saw me go inside?

Would I hear about it at work?

Would anyone want to play with me today?

Would guys I played with before pretend they didn't know me?

Would I be able to get—and keep—an erection?

Would I ejaculate or would the good stuff go right into my bladder?

Would I be able to get the other guy off?

What if he didn't like my hand job?

What if someone tried to grab my ass and I farted?

Tommy was right. I carried two dominant alleles for the worry gene.

Then there was the big question of the day. Was I a terrible, weak person because I was already going back on my agreement to postpone sex with strangers for two weeks? I'd told myself I'd just look today, not participate, but did that truly change the dynamics? Salvador probably didn't have sex the night he was killed. It was being here at all that was the problem, not orgasms.

I'd signed up for the break-down/clean-up shift today, not able to face the set-up shift after all the trauma from last time. I figured I might also go up front after Last Entry at 2:00 and monitor the front door for folks trying to get in late, which would also give me the opportunity to observe everyone leaving. I really wanted today to be about paying attention to other people.

If discovering a murderer was that easy, of course, detectives would have a much higher arrest rate.

Downstairs, a new rug was set out in front of the lockers. Distracted, I almost forgot to remove my Do Not Resuscitate necklace, needing to return to my locker before I headed upstairs.

Only six men were in the playroom when I sat down. As a rule, no one interacted at these events until twenty or more people arrived, either too nervous when unable to hide in a crowd or, more likely, afraid of missing out on a better looking man almost certainly due to arrive at any moment.

This afternoon, the room filled up quickly. There was a semi-regular with scoliosis, a beefy black guy, and a white man with a stomach so huge neither he nor anyone else could see his dick. The guy walked around without any apparent embarrassment. That alone was pleasant to witness. Some good looking men wore green wrist bands, happy to be touched by anyone, even the less traditionally attractive men. Several of the less attractive men rarely agreed to be touched by other less attractive men.

Sometimes, I felt I was negotiating an international treaty. As faulty as spoken language could be, I was impressed by how much we tried to communicate via glances and body posture.

Where were the subtitles when you needed them?

I stayed where I was and watched the men around me. In the dim light, I couldn't see what was happening on the far side of the room, but the guys near me hesitantly approached one another, gave each other hesitant glances, reached out hesitantly to touch a nipple or arm for permission, and hesitantly grasped each other's dicks.

One man, probably around forty, with short, dark blond hair, came up the stairs from the dressing room and strode confidently over to a striking Asian man around thirty. They didn't appear to know each other, but the white man took the Asian man's hand and placed it on his cock, and the affable Asian man started jacking the white guy off.

There was no reciprocation, but the Asian man didn't seem to mind.

It truly was delightful to see all of this in person. Video was fine, lots of fun, too, but you really couldn't beat watching men have a good time right in front of your face. It wasn't long before the subtle blend of sweat and semen began wafting through the air.

I'd spent a fortune one Christmas ordering a small bottle of semen-scented perfume for Tommy from a company in Paris. Even understanding how weird my gift was, it still hurt my feelings when he refused to wear it on Date Night. I wasn't even sure if he had the bottle any longer. I didn't know where it was, and I wasn't about to go looking through his things.

A man with several tattoos diagramming various molecules walked by, stopping near a column a few feet away. Since the neurons recording my chemistry classes were losing more synapses every day, I couldn't make out which molecules they were. I finally stood and walked over to the guy.

"Chocolate?" I asked, pointing to one of the tattoos. "Vanilla?" If I remembered correctly, fructose was the sugar found in semen.

"This one's salicylic acid," he replied, pointing to a design on his right forearm. Olive skin, which wasn't anywhere close to the color of olives, but which I still wanted to lick. "This one's capsaicin." He pointed to his left forearm. Insulin was on his right upper arm, penicillin on his left upper arm. Antihistamine was visible on his right calf.

"I'm not sure what to put on my left leg yet."

Years ago, I'd wanted to have "More, please!" tattooed on my ass, but Tommy said he'd divorce me. A few years later, he finally relented and allowed me to get "ti stubš" on one cheek and "ʔi" on the other. He told me it meant, "Men Yes," and I had to take his word for it.

Better than "yes men," I supposed, though I had no idea what Lushootseed connotations were.

I'd never been fucked by another Duwamish man, so Tommy was the only guy who knew for sure what my ass said. And I'd never gotten another tattoo in any language. Those things hurt.

But I was a fan of subtitles, so…

"It's my version of *Fahrenheit 451*," the molecule man told me. "I'm recording useful medications in case our health institutions collapse."

"Anything on your ass?" I asked.

He turned around and let me examine the blank slate. "Suggestions?"

"Petroleum jelly?"

"Not a medication. And a hydrocarbon chain's way too long."

We chatted a bit more, and then he moved on to join three men hugging and kissing each other near the padded cube.

Chris stopped by, already spent elsewhere, and we chatted briefly before he wandered off as well. Most of the regulars were here, scattered across the playroom. Clayton, of course. And Pranav and Marin and Stu and Jelani and a few others I recognized but whose names I'd never learned.

Most of the men didn't want to have an orgasm too quickly because they enjoyed being here and didn't want to leave. Instead, they flitted from dick to dick like bees gathering pollen. A few strokes of this dick, a few strokes of that dick, and on and on throughout the room.

This afternoon, though, I noticed frustrated men as often as those having a good time.

And then I saw Peter Cross. "Oh my god!" I said, putting my hand on his arm as he walked by. "Is that you?"

Peter turned to look, frowning. "Bruce? I hardly recognize you with your clothes off."

A pity. Since we'd known each other as coworkers at a previous job, I'd never asked him to play. Too risky. He was around fifty, bald, with a trim salt and pepper beard, wearing a smile that never looked forced. "How long's it been?" He'd lost a couple of pounds and looked pretty good, though I'd liked him just fine a few pounds heavier, too.

"A while." He told me about employees I'd known, briefly covered his bout with Stage One skin cancer, and explained he'd broken up with his partner a little over a year ago.

I expressed my condolences and asked how he was doing now.

"Planning a move to Seoul."

"Really?"

"Itaewon district, if possible."

Peter had friendly eyes. I couldn't keep myself from quickly surveying the rest of him while we chatted, despite the serious topics. His short chest hairs were salt and pepper, too. As were his pubic hairs, thankfully not trimmed like so many folks preferred these days. But if he was moving away, even this fortuitous reunion might not lead to a closer friendship.

Why hadn't I kept in touch after we were no longer coworkers? *Why* did so many of us keep throwing opportunities away? I tried to flick my red wrist band like a rubber band, but it was too thick to sting instructively.

"What can I say?" He chuckled. "I love K-pop and Korean TV shows."

How did I not know this about him? We'd worked together for two years. But then, that was almost ten years ago. Had I been watching European shows back then?

"And you speak Korean?"

He shrugged. "Getting better at it. I started studying harder a year ago when it looked like the election might not go well. I'm hoping to move in March."

Well after the incoming president promised to become a dictator on Day One.

I remembered it was against club rules to spend too much time talking. Conversation sucked testosterone out of the air. Even if the talkers were okay with that, the other guys weren't. I memorized Peter's phone number, though, and debated whether trading hand jobs with a former coworker constituted sex with a stranger. Before I could come to a decision, Peter leaned over and whispered in my ear.

"I want more than a quickie with you. Think we could get together sometime this week?"

"Absolutely."

"I'm poz," he said, "but undetectable."

"Top or bottom?" I asked.

"Both."

"Excellent!"

"No, but above average."

We chatted just a moment longer, and then I headed to the bathroom to pee before heading down to the dressing room. Almost time to start monitoring the front door. Since making a tentative date with Peter felt just as good as a hand job, I felt no temptation to play anymore this afternoon.

Marin was at the urinal when I came in. There was another urinal right beside his, but while I didn't have a shy prostate, I did have a shy kidney. I hesitated, wondering if I should head into the lone stall.

"I won't molest you," Marin said in a dead tone, looking over his shoulder. He shook off a couple of drops and turned to me. I was comfortable with quite a large variety of body types, but Marin's wasn't one of them.

"I weigh almost three hundred pounds," he said. "I know it's dark in the club, but even this skin can't be *that* invisible in the shadows."

I remembered what Chris had told me last night. "Rough day?"

Marin's eyes narrowed slightly. "Men don't look at me," he said. "So they won't need to turn me down." I could see one last drop on the tip of his penis. "If our eyes meet, they're convinced I want them. That I think we've signed a contract obligating them to touch me." He gave me a look. "And they'd rather die than touch me."

He motioned at his corpulent body like Vanna White before the puzzle board.

Had he emphasized the word "die" or had I imagined it?

It wasn't as if Marin *never* got to play. Chris and at least a couple of other guys had sex with him on occasion. Of course, I got to play, too. It was the looks the non-players gave that could still be devastating, as if you were a speck of feces on the condom you were pulling out of someone's ass.

I'd seen that look, with the slightly curled lip, directed toward me plenty of times. I could only imagine how often Marin saw the expression if he felt the need to talk about it.

"They don't want to be 'rude,'" he said. "After all, that's 'against club rules.'" He gave a disgusted snort. "So they ignore me. Pretend I don't exist. Because *that* isn't rude."

What could one say when there was nothing useful to say? "I'm…sorry you have to deal with that."

His eyes narrowed again. "I don't want your pity," he hissed.

I took a breath. There was a reason people avoided awkward conversations. This was a damned if you do, damned if you don't moment, like far too many involving interpersonal interaction. Men in our culture were bad at this. Even "sensitive" gay men. And there were sure a lot of insensitive gay jerks, too.

I might well be one of them.

"Caring isn't pity," I said. Though, to be fair, I hardly knew the guy, so my ability to care for him specifically was limited. Still, I could care about the overall injustice of the situation. "But even if you equate the two, why bother telling anyone what's hurt you if you're hoping they don't care?"

"Maybe I'm trying to decide who to kill next." Marin plodded toward the door, a listless, no energy trudge out of the bathroom.

Not the walk of a killer.

At least, none of the murderers on *Tatort: Dortmund* had ever walked like that. Not on *Cherif*, either.

This was why people wanted sex with no strings attached. With anonymous sex, even with most casual sex encounters, you didn't need to deal with the full person. And full people were nothing if not complicated. Most of us, Tommy and I included, were also damaged in one way or another. Often in multiple ways.

Gays just want to have fu-uhn, I sang to myself in Cyndi Lauper's voice.

Still, despite everything, being out in the world meeting people was *interesting*. I liked it.

Though I was definitely looking forward to seeing my husband's asshole again when I got home.

I turned back toward the urinal and pissed. I was right in the middle of a weak stream when suddenly someone put their hands over my eyes and pulled me back.

Chapter Twelve

"Guess who?" Whoever it was held me close against them. The guy had a bit of a tummy and seemed to be flaccid, not really enough to go on. But this wasn't a game, not here, not after last time. Trying to remember one of my self-defense videos, I pulled away, swirled around quickly, and grabbed the man's wrists.

"Stu!" Apparently, shoddy self-defense moves worked if the other person wasn't a real threat.

"I washed my hands," Stu said. "Promise!" He wiggled his fingers, the only part of his hands still free.

"Porca la miseria."

"Come on," he said. "Hurry up. I need to pee."

I released Stu's wrists and stepped aside.

"No, no," he said. "Sit on the toilet."

"Excuse me?"

He pointed into the stall without a door. "Sit and spread your legs. I promise I can aim between them."

It was hard to claim that *other* gay men were weird when I was also here at this mass sex event. But whatever. I didn't need to be into something myself to help someone else have a good time. Being a prop wasn't hurting me any. I sat on the toilet as far back as I could manage and spread my legs. Stu smiled and stepped up, a gleam in his eyes as he took aim.

I kept quiet as his stream began, not wanting to throw him off course. Seeing his satisfaction was satisfying. I could get off simply on that, even if the act itself did little for me.

When he finally finished, a few last drops hit my leg.

"Oops," he said.

"I've had the cum of three different men on me at one time in this club," I said. "A little piss isn't going to hurt me."

Stu's smile turned wistful. "Thanks, Bruce," he said. "I wish…" He didn't finish the statement, and I didn't pursue it. Chris had enjoyed fucking Stu, but Stu was another guy who wasn't really my type.

Perhaps I was pickier than I thought.

I'd jacked off a Latino guy here one night who'd walked away with a lube cup stuck between his ass cheeks. Obese guys weren't usually my type, either, but chemistry was chemistry. You could never tell who was going to turn you on until you gave it a shot.

"Salvador used to make fun of me," Stu said. "Used to mock what he called my 'pencil dick.' But I decided that the best defense was a good offense. Only good thing I ever got from my dad forcing me to watch sports."

The only good thing I ever got from sports was asking Gaetano, one of the local church members in Rome, to play soccer with the missionaries. He'd tripped once and fallen on top of me. I *still* replayed that scene sometimes when I beat off, forty-five years later.

"So at the last event, when Sal came up to me in the locker room, before he could even open his mouth, I said, 'You still need two dick pills to get hard?'"

"And what did he say?" I asked, not pleased he considered this an insult. For obvious reasons.

"He told me to get the fuck out of his sight. And I did. I made some other comment about leaving my mark on two guys earlier with my bold permanent marker dick and headed back up the stairs and out of the building." Stu shuddered. "Salvador must have been killed within minutes of that conversation." He hugged himself, rubbing his arms for warmth. "I can't help but wonder if he'd still be alive if I hadn't been so quick with my tongue for once."

I couldn't quite remember what Chris had told me about this interaction, only that Stu's account felt off.

"I've been completely freaked out ever since the murder," I said truthfully before adding a lie. "I even went out to buy a gun."

"You know how to shoot?"

I shook my head. "Not really." I waited for Stu to say something about the gun I knew he'd bought, but he didn't. Should I bring it up? Ask point blank? Watch his reaction?

Would that help or hurt my amateur investigation? "Do you?" I asked.

"Oh, goodness no," he said. "Guns scare me."

Technically, they scared me, too. Didn't mean I didn't own one.

Stu sighed. "Well, I've cum and I've pissed, so I guess I'd better get home." He leaned down to kiss my forehead. "Um…"

"Yes?"

"You don't seem totally into this…"

"Not especially."

"But would you be up to coming over and pissing on me sometime?"

"Nope," I said. I didn't even need to think about it. Stu's face fell, but I kept talking. "I'm on public transit," I explained. "That's a lot of work for something I'm not that into. But if you want to come to my place sometime, just give me a heads up, and I'll drink a big glass of water first. With my prostate, I'll be ready to burst by the time you ring the bell."

Well, ready to dribble.

"I'm having a lot more fun today than I had last time."

I should hope so. But then, he did leave before the murder, so he probably had a better time than at least sixty other men that evening.

We walked downstairs together to the locker room, where we exchanged phone numbers as we dressed. I walked back up with him and gave him a hug in the foyer. "You're staying?" he asked.

"I'm on clean-up crew tonight."

"I'll give you a call."

I stood beside a chest-high end table and began nodding at folks as they left. I'd heard Clayton talking about possibly creating a new volunteer position whose only assignment would be monitoring after Last Entry. But it seemed a herculean task filling the spots already needed. As it was, I'd only managed to get up here at 2:10, so the door had already been unmonitored for ten minutes. For most events, it went unmonitored altogether after the check-in crew pulled off their jock straps and joined folks in the playroom.

Most of the men nodding goodbye had no clue I was a volunteer. If I didn't recognize them, they almost certainly didn't recognize me. But because I looked official, many thanked me before heading out, as if I was responsible for the event. I was happy to accept the unearned gratitude.

Around 2:30, a man tried to enter as someone exited. The door could only be opened from the inside, but every once in a while, people seemed to be waiting for someone to leave so they could slip in before the door closed again. This time, it was an elderly Asian man speaking Chinese. The only word

I thought I could make out was "pizza." I shook my head and ushered him back out the door.

I returned to the end table and swayed to the music.

"Bruce!" Clayton gave me a sweaty bear hug as he came around the curtain. "Always good to see you. Let me know how clean-up goes."

I nodded. He didn't say anything about my jumping into the role of Door Monitor today, but I wasn't looking for brownie points, just something to do until the event was over.

"If you like this job better, I might train you to be one of our closing managers."

One step at a time, please. I hugged Clayton again, inhaling his scent. Despite the club rules, he had *not* washed the night's cum off his body. Or he'd bought a bottle of the same perfume I'd given Tommy.

Damn, he smelled good. That hint of sweat mixed in made him downright lickable.

There were no other huggers on the way out. Ofer, the Israeli guy, asked for my phone number. So did Owen, who I'd never even spoken with before. He was in his fifties, with dark hair in a buzz cut, two nipple rings, and three stainless steel spikes with subcutaneous bases protruding from his right forearm. I sure hoped he wasn't into fisting.

I'd never been this popular even in my twenties, and never before at JOB. I couldn't help but wonder if these men were truly interested or were trying to determine what I knew about Salvador.

The minutes passed by pleasantly. Someone knocked on the door. Turned out he'd left his phone, so I let him back in to check the locker room. He came back upstairs a few minutes later, waved the phone at me, and turned it on, revealing a photo of two young girls as his screen saver.

Nieces? Daughters? Not everyone here was gay or bi.

A man unlocked his bicycle parked in the lobby and headed out. He was followed a moment later by a man who had to be in his nineties.

Pranav frowned at me as he passed on his way out. A shame, as he was damn hot. But I had plenty to work with already, so it was all good. I really, really wanted Tommy to feel better about himself. It was a blast interacting sexually with other men. And I loved him. So I wanted *him* to have—

A scream pierced the air, louder even than the music playing in the playroom. The first scream was followed by another, then by several shouts.

Oh my god. Not again. Surely, someone had just slipped. Had a heart attack. Some kind of normal injury.

Maybe someone had pissed on a man who didn't want to be pissed on.

The lights came up and the music stopped. David, the Mark Spitz lookalike, ran up to the front. "Bruce. Don't let anyone else out. I called 9-1-1. We've got another murder."

Cazzo! "Who?" I hadn't seen Chris leave yet. Or Jelani. Was Marin still here? Tuyen?

David shook his head. "Don't know the guy. We get almost ten new men at every function. Look, I gotta get back there." He shot off toward the playroom. "Call Clayton!" he shouted as he disappeared.

I felt anchored to the front door, frustrated I couldn't go see what was happening. Two men I vaguely recognized forced their way past me. I could hardly blame them. And I certainly wasn't going to stop them. They didn't look like murderers, just very scared men.

Was Peter still here? I'd been in the bathroom so long with Marin and Stu that he could have left before I took up my position in the foyer. The poor man would never come back if this was his first experience.

A cold shiver ran through me, despite the warmth.

Peter wasn't the new guy killed, was he? I pulled out my phone and called but there was no answer. Of course, if he was driving, he wouldn't be able to pick up. If he was home, he might not have his phone on him.

I shot Clayton a two-word message. "Another murder!"

Then I texted Tommy, barely finishing two sentences before I heard the sirens approaching.

"I've got news, too," I saw him reply just as two officers burst through the door.

Chapter Thirteen

Two officers herded twenty-seven men into the playroom while four others secured the exits. Because today's event had been scheduled for a Saturday afternoon, we'd started out with a larger crowd than usual, but because the murder had taken place so late in the event, most participants had already left. The officers began allowing a few men at a time into the locker room to get dressed before Detectives Altan and Downey arrived. The others seemed already used to grabbing linens off the chairs while waiting for their turn.

Detective Downey wore bright blue braids today, reminding me of Amanita from *Sense8*.

Detective Altan caught my eye but didn't give any other indication that we were "friends." How he kept his nine o'clock shadow pencil beard always at nine o'clock was intriguing. Did he trim it during every bathroom break?

"Who's in charge here?" Detective Downey asked.

A tall black man raised his hand. "I'm the closing manager." I realized I didn't have any clue who the guy was, hadn't even known he was in charge of the clean-up crew tonight. I made a note to talk to Clayton about it. In addition to a binder with laminated instructions for set-up and breakdown, we needed a procedure to introduce the closing crew to the manager when we arrived, so we knew who to turn to when it was time to get to work. Make this part of the check-in process when we arrived.

Was this *really* what I was going to worry about right now?

I stole a glance at Demir, remembering our conversation in the park about why he'd chosen to speak to me in person. And I suddenly experienced a flashback to the time my missionary companion and I did a radio show in Quartu. We'd somehow convinced a local station to give us half an hour of airtime for free each week. We agreed to play a certain number of pop songs but could say whatever we wanted in between songs.

Anziano Archer and I took turns reading from the first missionary discussion in Italian, which for some reason was C, not A. And we'd queue up songs we recognized for the breaks. "Then Joseph Smith knelt in the grove to pray, where he was visited by God the Father and Jesus Christ." I could still recite all eight lessons from start to finish in Italian.

Next, Barbra Streisand would croon, "I'm just a woman in love…"

When the song finished, we'd get back to what Joseph Smith learned during that visitation.

And then Ricchi e Poveri would sing, "Sarà perché ti amo!"

We'd follow that by talking about the Angel Moroni. It was against mission rules to watch TV or read newspapers. Or listen to the radio, for that matter, but we could hear pop songs on the jukebox at the train station or coming from our neighbor's apartment.

We were probably being filmed for some prank show, the Italian equivalent of *Candid Camera*, and never knew.

Focus, Bruce, focus.

Eric, the closing manager, was the first to look at a photo of the man who'd been murdered in the bathroom and shook his head. "I don't recognize him."

Detective Altan moved about the room, showing the photo to each man in turn. No one seemed to know who the guy was. Demir had shown the photo to fifteen men before he got a hit.

"I don't know him either," Chris said, "but I saw Bruce talking to the guy for a while."

"Uh…"

All heads turned toward me as Chris pointed. "But they weren't arguing!" Chris insisted. "I know Bruce. He wouldn't hurt a fly!"

Actually, I did hang up fly traps in the house every spring. Tommy had a bad habit of leaving the back door open when he worked in the yard.

Focus, Bruce!

Detective Altan walked over to me, showing me the photo. "It's…it's Peter Cross," I managed. Oh my god. "We used to work together at my previous job. This was his first time at the club."

And his last.

I could see marks around Peter's throat. It looked like he'd been strangled. The floor tiles underneath him looked like those in the bathroom.

"Were you on good terms with the victim?" Detective Downey asked.

"With Peter," I corrected. "We weren't really on *any* terms. We hadn't spoken in years."

"So on bad terms then?" she pressed.

I understood what she was doing and managed not to feel irked. "We lost touch," I said. "We were never friends outside of work, and when I got a new job, we no longer had a reason to talk to each other."

"Why did you leave that job?" Detective Downey asked.

"Because I didn't enjoy being a loan officer. I hate sales, and my boss kept raising my 'goals' every month." *Way* too much like the Standard of Excellence on my mission.

"So…a disgruntled former employee?" She asked several more questions about our history, what we talked about this afternoon, our plans to meet up later. Altan threw in another couple of questions about our proposed encounter as well. Then Detective Downey asked even more questions, but there really wasn't much to add. I did tell them about the two men who'd run out after the murder, but since I couldn't give a detailed description, I wasn't sure they even believed it had happened at all.

"You've had close interaction with two of the victims," Detective Downey pointed out.

"I've had close interaction with a lot of the men here," I pointed out in return.

She nodded. "Since we're considering the possibility of a serial killer, the fact that you may have only killed two people so far isn't exactly an alibi."

"We realize you were up front in the lobby," Detective Altan stated nonchalantly, looking at his partner rather than at me as he said it, "but the murderer could be working with someone else."

Like those two men who ran! I wanted to shout.

The lead detective's gaze never left my face. "That could help explain how someone could kill two people at a crowded event and not be discovered."

Did it, though? I still wouldn't have been able to keep anyone from going into the bathroom and stumbling upon the murder as it happened.

Fortunately, the detectives moved on to the next interview, and I grabbed a stray linen and wiped my face. The fabric smelled like men.

I was struck again by how odd it felt to be part of what seemed a mass interrogation. Was this typical? Were there just too many people to schlep over to the police department? Was this some kind of psychological attempt to make us feel less defensive, hoping we'd give something away? A way to make us feel *more* pressure?

Even most of the detective shows I watched were set in Europe, not the U.S., so I really didn't know what was or wasn't normal. In shows like *Imma Tataranni*, the prosecutor herself did the detective work.

Unless those shows weren't accurate for Italian audiences, either.

Perhaps Detectives Downey and Altan were flagrantly breaking rules.

I thought again about the conversation I'd had with Demir at the park.

It appeared that Stu, Clayton, Pranav, and Marin had all left before the murder took place—or at least before it had been discovered—so they'd be questioned later. The detectives questioned Andrew, one of Salvador's exes, who said he hadn't noticed Peter today. With only twenty-seven men left at the end, that seemed unlikely, but guys could certainly be super focused when it came to sex, so who knew?

"Do you know if this guy had a life insurance policy?" Andrew asked.

Detective Downey raised an eyebrow.

Andrew shrugged. "It's one of the reasons I broke up with Sal," he explained. "He'd taken out a life insurance policy on me without my permission, and I didn't feel safe around him anymore."

"Did you feel safe around him here at the club?" Detective Altan asked.

He shrugged again.

"No feeling you needed to defend yourself?" Detective Altan continued.

Andrew frowned. "Weren't we talking about this Peter guy?" he asked.

"We're investigating *two* murders," Detective Downey reminded him.

The questioning dragged on a while longer, though not as long as it had the first time. It wasn't until the detectives reached the second-to-last man that another clue popped up.

"Clue" was probably a word only amateurs used.

One man in his early thirties, Jamie, said he'd talked to Peter half an hour before his body was discovered. "He'd seemed irritated," Jamie said. "Something about having run into someone he knew and not being happy about it."

Several heads turned to look in my direction.

"Did he say why he was unhappy?" Detective Downey asked.

Jamie shook his head. "Nothing specific, only that the guy seemed 'shady.'"

I surveyed the room and saw several men staring at me suspiciously. I was about to say something when Chris suddenly jumped in. "Bruce may be a lot of things, but shady isn't one of them." He chuckled. "It could all be an act, but no one would mistake him for being shady, that's for sure." He shook his head. "No, this guy was talking about someone else." He paused and looked at me a long moment, his brows furrowing. "Of course…"

"Yes?" asked Detective Downey.

Chris looked at her, then at me, and back at her. "Nothing."

What the hell was *that* about? I looked over at Demir, who was looking back at me intently. I realized I must have quite an unhappy look on my face right now, certainly nothing that screamed, "Innocent!"

"What's the motive behind all this?" I asked. "Someone trying to make gay men look like degenerates? Why bother? People who want to believe that already do. But there's no connection other than the club."

"And you." The detectives exchanged a glance.

Tommy had asked me not to come back until Salvador's murder was solved.

"What if," I said, "Peter was the real target all along, and Sal was only killed first to disguise that?" I tried to run with the idea, though I wasn't sure it made me look any less guilty. "Maybe Peter told someone he was thinking of coming to the club, and that person decided to make Peter the second victim so it would look more random."

Detective Altan's eyes widened at the suggestion while Detective Downey's eyes narrowed.

"Maybe," I said, "*neither* of them is the real target. Maybe the person who's got a tie to the murderer is the *next* victim."

Now it was Eric's turn to glower at me. I'd just scared off every man here from coming to the next event, and probably telling their friends about it, too. If I wasn't a target before, I might well be now.

"Maybe," Detective Downey said, "the murderer is trying to throw us off track by bringing up wild scenarios."

There was a long silence. Then a man sitting on the padded cube raised his hand.

Detective Downey motioned toward him. "Yes?" she asked, sounding slightly peeved.

"No one's interviewed me yet," he said.

The lead detective looked at him a moment longer before speaking. "And what do you know about Peter Cross?" she asked.

"Nothing at all. Never saw him before and didn't speak with him today."

Detective Downey looked ready to slap the guy.

No matter who the detectives suspected, they probably couldn't keep anyone in a cell for more than twenty-four hours before being forced to either release or arrest them. I could be going about my life thinking they weren't even looking into my background and then suddenly find myself facing a pair of handcuffs the instant they felt they had something incriminating.

Over the next couple of days, the detectives would be searching frantically for some connection between Salvador and Peter. Was someone knocking off all the members of a gay book club that had disbanded years ago? Perhaps they'd both dated the same guy who was now dying of cancer and had decided to take everyone he'd ever been with along for the journey.

"Needle in a haystack" was a cliché, but I understood better now why it had been coined.

Chris was already way better at this private investigating than I was ever going to be.

Detective Downey nodded, blinking her eyes slowly as if beyond ready for the day to be over. She did not slap the man. Instead, she motioned to the men in the playroom while looking at her watch. "Everyone can head out now. Just know we'll probably be following up with more questions later."

"Wait!" Eric said.

"Yes?"

"The closing crew still needs to clean up so the art gallery can open tomorrow." He pointed to four of us in the crowd. "Let's get going, guys."

The detectives, and everyone else except the closers and the remaining forensics team, quickly shuffled out of the building. Demir didn't even say goodbye.

Chapter Fourteen

I texted Tommy on my way home, not up to a phone call about murder while riding light rail, though a perverse part of me wouldn't have minded freaking out the blond family heading with their luggage to the airport. The mother already looked terrified to be sitting near an East African immigrant wearing a gauzy white shawl who she probably didn't realize was every bit as Christian as her family.

Cleaning up the playroom after the event had not been a pleasant experience, but then, setting up last time with Salvador hadn't been so hot, either. I did, at least, get a chance to talk briefly with Eric, the closing manager.

"Clayton told me to keep an eye out for trouble," he said, "and I botched it."

I handed him a tub filled with containers of alcohol wipes, and he hoisted it on top of the lockers. "You can't follow seventy people around every second of the event," I reassured him.

He shrugged. "Didn't need to be seventy. Clayton had a short list of possible troublemakers."

My ears pricked up. "Any names you feel comfortable sharing?" I struggled to lift a heavy tub of padlocks and handed it to Eric, who placed the tub on top of the lockers with no hesitation.

He laughed. "Yours, for one."

I sputtered but couldn't find words to respond.

"Pranav opens the little cups of lube and deliberately tosses them on the floor. Sorrel sometimes grabs a cup of water from the dispenser and beats off into it. Then he leaves the cup on a table, hoping someone will accidentally drink from it. And Baylor likes to sniff the artwork while he beats off."

I had no idea who Baylor was. But I really needed to hang around Sorrel on my next visit. The name sounded familiar, but I couldn't quite place him. Was he the guy with maroon hair?

So many men, so many names and faces and quirks to remember. I needed to find a nice, small group of men, perhaps ten guys who wanted to watch foreign movies together at each other's homes, and just play within that group. Something manageable, moderate. Ten was a reasonable number of sex buddies, right?

"So…not all the troublemakers are murder suspects?"

"Clayton's threatened Baylor a couple of times, so more likely a murder victim if he doesn't shape up."

I couldn't tell if Eric was joking, since the subject seemed beyond jokeable at this point, but I decided he was.

No other information I heard from him or the others on the clean-up crew seemed relevant. Even that discussion showed I was apparently the only actual suspect on Clayton's list. I almost felt flattered. I couldn't often pull off "suspicious." Once, a man in Rome had opened his door with a gun pointed at me, saying he thought my companion and I were only pretending to be missionaries. When he finally believed us, he sent us to his neighbor next door, who we later learned he didn't like.

Old people had way too many anecdotes to keep track of.

I supposed, in a murder investigation, the least suspicious person often became the most suspicious, just because of all the movies we'd seen.

"The butler did it!" wasn't even true in most murders, but it did have a better ring than "The volunteer for the clean-up crew did it!"

I hugged Tommy for almost five minutes when I got home. Finally, he pulled back. "I don't have to say it, do I?"

I shook my head. "I won't go back until the murders are solved."

Even as I promised him, though, I wondered if I could arrive for the next event after playtime was completely over and the only part left was cleaning up. I still wanted to participate with the group, still wanted to contribute in some way, still wanted to keep this tiny sliver of gay culture alive.

A Mormon senator from Utah, so repulsive I was surprised even other Mormons liked him, wanted to pass a federal law banning all porn. But for him, that also included the casual mention of any LGBTQ people. No one would be able to cast a gay best friend on a sitcom. No Broadway shows like *Angels in America*. Websites like Lambda Legal or the Human Rights Campaign would be criminalized. Even Log Cabin Republicans couldn't exist. Under the new administration, he might finally succeed.

No need to worry about a propaganda law if we were deemed porn instead.

"Resistance is local." I couldn't fight in every battle. But I could fight for *this*.

I quickly summarized what had happened at the club and then asked Tommy the question I should have asked as soon as I got home. "And what happened here? You said something happened here."

"I found the front door unlocked when I came back from the gym," he said. Tommy usually left the house through the rear door, and I usually left through the front. No particular reason, just personal preference. I'd come home several times to discover the back door unlocked but occasionally found the front door unlocked at other times, too.

"Damn," I said. "Did I forget? Did anyone come in?" It was ridiculous in this day and age to be so careless, irresponsible not to have a security system. But an unlocked door hardly seemed to warrant his text.

"I don't *think* anyone came in," Tommy said.

"Why the hesitation?"

"The refrigerator door was slightly ajar."

I could feel myself frowning. Surely, neither of us would do something like that. But then, sometimes I found the microwave ajar while we were both home. No one else could possibly have touched it. So who knew?

Had someone poisoned an item of food in the fridge? If we got sick, would it be from the food temperature not having been kept cold enough or from something else?

Had the egg thrower from the other night come inside?

"Nothing else seemed disturbed."

Was one of us developing dementia? Was this why I felt unfocused so often?

I'd asked Tommy to find a way to kill me without it looking like murder if I ever got to a point where I couldn't think normally. He'd said, rightfully so, that it was too big a burden to place on him. He promised to "go swimming in the Sound" if he started developing dementia. But I'd read articles that suggested people kept putting off that final decision until things got a little worse, and by the time things really did get that bad, they were no longer in a position to take action.

That was another reason I'd purchased the gun.

I asked Tommy for a few minutes to check my emails, and while in my office I verified that my pistol was still hidden where I'd put it. I'd just closed a cabinet when

Tommy knocked on the door. "You ready?" he said, pulling his shirt off and sniffing his armpits.

I'd forgotten, but I could feel myself hardening as I remembered our arrangement. I jumped up and followed him to the bathroom, where I watched him finish stripping and step into the shower. My god, he was a good looking man. His face had become a bit more padded in recent years, and he now sported a deep horizontal crease across the bridge of his nose, but the absolute uniformity of salt and pepper coloring on top of his head, in his sideburns, his beard, his moustache, and even his eyebrows was a sight to behold.

Even the few strands of hair around his asshole were salt and pepper, three or four grains of each. I sat on the toilet after he dried off and asked him to lean forward over the counter. I pried his cheeks apart and stared.

"You okay back there?" he finally asked.

I chuckled. "I suppose it's odd to find assholes beautiful, and I guess I don't find all of them attractive, but yours sure is."

"You are *not* taking a picture."

"Not even to use as a model for my next quilt design?"

"Just rim me already."

I buried my face in his crack, and we kept at that for a good ten minutes. I didn't want to push my luck, though, and was just about to pull back when Tommy straightened up, forcing me out. "Drop your pants," he ordered.

"Really?"

"I don't want you to go back to the club for a while, and you're going to need some sex in the meantime."

Oh.

I wanted sex with Tommy because he was sexy and because I loved him. I wasn't sure I wanted it as a safety precaution. But perhaps we could prime the pump so that the water might start flowing more freely from here on out. I pulled off my pants and underwear while Tommy grabbed some hair conditioner. Within seconds, I could feel the tip of his penis against my sphincter, and within just a few more seconds, he was all the way inside.

I groaned. Damn, that hurt. That head of his was *big*.

"You like it?"

Absolutely. "Ride this curelom," I said, slapping the side of my ass.

Tommy's dick featured the darkest skin on his body, with the tip shaped like the cap on a portabella mushroom. Shortly after we first began dating, while he was recounting some of his religious trauma, he'd told me, "Roses be damned. During *my* last days, I want to spore like a mushroom."

"Jesus Christ, Bruce. You are a piece of work." But he fucked me. Hard. And his own groan when he came sounded full of pleasure.

After dinner, Tommy and I played a game of Scrabble. He turned my "phony" into "symphony," my "racy" into "piracy" and then "conspiracy." He turned my "aging" into "savaging," my "tent" to "stent."

I'm not revealing the final score.

After I put the game away, we held hands on the sofa while we watched an episode of *Unseen*, a Belgian show about people who disappear, with actors filmed naked for the scenes where viewers see things from their perspective. I was just nodding off when Tommy nudged me.

"Your phone's ringing."

I usually didn't answer my phone at night. I hadn't set up voice mail but figured people could either text or I'd see their number and call them back at another time. Given the chaos of the past couple of weeks, though, I thought I'd better check.

"Hey, Demir," I said, catching him just in time. "I mean, Detective Altan."

"Demir's fine," he replied. "I had to keep my distance at the club, but I know you didn't have anything to do with this. We just need to be thorough for when we build our case against the guy who *is* responsible."

"I don't expect you can give me a name yet," I said, "but do you at least have a good suspect? I probably didn't take the first murder as seriously as I should have because Salvador was such a creep. But Peter was a good guy."

"Murder is like catching a plane to Istanbul," Demir said.

"Okay."

"It sounds like a far off, distant, mystical place, but in just a few hours, even if you've never left your hometown until you were twenty, you can be there and discover it's all completely real." He paused. "And amazingly easy to reach."

"I'm not sure what—"

"Anyone can kill, Bruce," Demir said. "I bet I've already worked on more murder cases than you've been on planes in your entire life."

It was an odd analogy, but I understood his point.

"Don't go back to the club," he said. "And don't meet up with anyone you know from there until this is over."

"But—"

"No one," he repeated. "I mean it."

He wished me a good night, said he probably wouldn't be able to meet with me this week, encouraged me to keep seeing the therapist he'd referred me to, and promised me a good time when this was all over.

Just having the murder solved would constitute a good time, as far as I was concerned.

"The detective?" Tommy asked when I hung up. He hadn't been eavesdropping, but it would have been impossible not to hear some of that conversation.

"He said I should invest more energy into *our* relationship." I grabbed his hand. "So if you're okay with it, I'm going to brush, floss, and gargle. And then we're going to kiss for fifteen minutes before I head to the sofa for the evening." It wasn't that I could predict a bad bout of sleep apnea. I simply needed time to cocoon.

Tommy's tongue wasn't as good as Chris's, but I missed it and was happy to get reacquainted. Tommy went the second mile and made sure our make-out session lasted five minutes beyond my goal.

What with the world falling apart and all, it had been a long time since I'd fallen asleep happy. Too weird that it happened on the day of the second murder, but choosing good things always mattered.

Not long after Tommy headed to his office, I received a text with a photo of Demir's living room. Two books on the end table beside the sofa, but I couldn't make out the titles. His lamp was in the shape of a redwood, the shade fashioned from dark green glass.

An hour after I'd gone to sleep, I was thrilled to wake up later as Tommy passed by on his way to the bedroom, stopping just long enough to wipe a handful of cum across my lips and cheeks, so I could remember his smell throughout the night.

Unfortunately, three hours later, the home invasion began.

Chapter Fifteen

I heard the footsteps first. Tommy had always slept more soundly than I did. And the bedroom had better insulation. Sleeping on the sofa in the living room, I could hear the refrigerator humming all night, could hear traffic on Renton Avenue, could sometimes even hear gunfire at the police shooting range over a mile away. I could hear neighborhood cats or raccoons or squirrels on the front porch or the back deck or on top of the AC window unit.

So when I heard the floorboards creak on the front porch, at first I barely noticed. Then I heard more creaks. And then I heard something out back.

Oh my god, I thought. This was it. The Proud Boys were coming for us. Or that group of Christian dominionists headquartered in Spokane. Maybe some random haters. Perhaps it was just run-of-the-mill thieves. There'd been a string of home invasions lately across the city but usually targeting Asian families.

What should I do?

My body produced more adrenalin over the next few seconds than it had in the previous three years combined. It was energizing—should I grab the coffee table like a battering ram and charge whoever came through the door?—

and paralyzing at the same time—What to do? What to do? What to do?

Someone pounded on the front door. *Bam! Bam! Bam!* "Police!" someone shouted. "Open up!"

But *was* it the police? Anyone could *say* they were the police. Was I going to open the door in the middle of the night to a bunch of angry men and carefully examine their IDs? Would I even recognize a counterfeit one in the first place?

I heard Tommy moaning and rustling the blankets in his sleep.

"Police!" the man out front shouted again. "Open the door now!"

If it was the police, and I resisted, I'd be shot. We'd all seen it on the news dozens of times. Even if I was spared, Tommy was indigenous. He'd be killed for sure.

If it wasn't the police, and I let them in, then what?

I felt a rogue wave of misanthropy wash over me. Humans were an awful species. I hoped we went extinct soon. Maybe the new administration would ban vaccines and bird flu would explode across the nation.

Perhaps Armageddon *was* the solution.

"Coming!" I shouted, standing up. I'd paid almost a thousand dollars for that door. As I passed the bedroom, I shouted in Tommy's direction. "Get up! The police are here!"

I turned the lights on and walked over to the front door. I unlocked it slowly, trying to give Tommy an extra few moments to throw on a bathrobe, since he slept naked. At least I had on my sweatpants and a T-shirt that read "United we bargain. Divided we beg," though the raised fist might look suspicious.

As soon as I finished turning the lock, several men wearing bulletproof vests and thick helmets swarmed into the living room, guns drawn. Were we being swatted? I raised my hands and stood motionless. Two men seemed to know exactly which was the bedroom and rushed in there. Another ran to the back door to let additional officers into the house. I stared at the bedroom door and held my breath but heard no gunshots.

The front door was wide open, cold air rushing inside. The temperature tonight was in the upper thirties. During the long winter months, I kept the heat on low in the living room overnight and slept under a warm blanket. Our electric bill was well over $400 as it was. But it meant that now I was shivering. Being nervous didn't help.

The men—I still wasn't convinced they were officers, though their gear looked impressive—pushed Tommy out of the bedroom to stand beside me, his arms raised as well. Neither of us spoke. We simply watched what was happening as two men rummaged about in my office and two others who'd just entered headed for Tommy's. I'd read that if police insisted on searching your home, you should call out to Alexa or Siri to record, but there was no way I was going to demand to see a warrant or risk angering these heavily armed men.

Intimidation was an effective tactic. It worked.

"Found a handgun," someone called out from my office.

Tommy turned to look at me. I remained silent.

Time seemed to function differently. On the one hand, everything seemed to happen in an instant. On the other, it felt as if the intrusion lasted hours. Tommy and I both eventually lowered our hands. But within half an hour, the men had carted off our computers, our cell phones, and my handgun. Since neither murder had been committed with a gun, the logic didn't make sense. But those were questions to be posed by an attorney later.

How the hell was I going to find an attorney? Or pay for one? Freedom wasn't really free if you couldn't afford it.

"Are we being detained?" I asked when there were only two officers left.

The man in charge looked at my T-shirt again, his lip curling slightly, and shook his head. Labor unions and police unions were two completely different things. While I'd known a couple of gay police officers who seemed like good guys and who swore they knew other officers who were good guys, it was the institution itself and lack of accountability that was the problem. Even when it was obvious an officer had killed an unarmed, innocent person who wasn't resisting, there were almost never any serious consequences.

I might like Demir, but I could never fully trust someone in his position.

And speaking of the devil…

The officer had just opened his mouth to reply when Detectives Downey and Altan walked through the door. Both looked a bit bleary eyed.

"Really?" I said. The huff that accompanied my question was usually described in subtitles in parentheses. (Scoffs.) "Whatever's going on here couldn't wait until morning?" I gritted my teeth. It was one thing to terrorize suspects, and it was clear I was back on that list, if I'd ever left it. But did the commanding officer really need to wake up the detectives handling the case? Their questions couldn't wait until daylight? In so many of the French detective shows we watched, the marriages of the main characters kept falling apart because the spouses could never rely on the detectives to keep hours that allowed a relationship to survive, much less thrive.

"We'll take it from here," Detective Downey told the officer. "Thanks." Then she turned to us. "We received an anonymous tip that you have a schematic on your computer for the art gallery where the sex club meets," she said, nodding at Tommy.

"Excuse me?" I said.

"With every possible exit marked."

I looked over at Tommy, whose face was completely expressionless.

"*Do* you have a map of the building?" she asked.

I continued to watch Tommy, whose face remained blank. At first, the thought of him looking up the layout of the club seemed odd, but then, why *wouldn't* he try to figure out if the layout made the place even more dangerous than I thought? He might have been planning to build a stronger case to keep me away, even if there hadn't been a second murder. But…

"Wait a second," I said. "Who in the world could possibly have called in such a tip?" I huffed again. "Even if it were true, and even if there weren't a perfectly innocent reason for having the map, how could anyone else possibly know what is or isn't on Tommy's computer?" I looked Detective Downey in the eyes now. "That 'tip' almost has to be from the killer himself. Are you tracking it down?"

I wondered if there really even was a tip. The detectives would have needed to offer the judge something to get a warrant, but someone in the department could probably have fabricated a tip.

What if someone was now *planting evidence* on one of our computers?

I gasped.

"What?" Detective Altan asked, his eyes narrowing. He was close enough now that I could see his nostrils flare slightly as he sniffed the air. I saw his eyes scan my cheeks and remembered Tommy's midnight gift.

Didn't we have the right to be 'freaky' in our own home?

I remembered *Bowers v. Hardwick* and knew those days were coming back soon enough.

"Someone came into our house this afternoon when we were both out," I said.

Tommy sighed, and I knew I should stop talking, but I couldn't help myself. Had someone been planning to come in and plant evidence ever since the first murder but hadn't had a chance until now? This might have been the first time we'd left the door unlocked during that period, at least when that person was also around to check.

Either Stu or Marin could have come to the house after leaving the club and before Tommy got home from the gym. I decided to share that information with Demir.

"Maybe," he said. "But your suspicion isn't enough to get a warrant to check their GPS or track their cell phone location over the past several hours."

"Yet an anonymous tip was enough to get us raided in the middle of the night?"

Tommy still hadn't said a word, and ultimately, the detectives couldn't really do much more questioning until their IT people checked out all the devices they'd taken. Detective Downey held up a plastic bag with more "evidence" taken from my office.

"A burner phone?" she asked, raising an eyebrow.

"It's not a burner phone!" I said, struggling not to sound as irritated as I felt. Tommy gave me another look. "It's just a phone."

"Uh huh."

It was the phone I'd had on me at the club, though I managed not to say so just before the words popped out of my mouth. "It's for hook ups," I explained. "I'm not going to give out my real cell phone number to a complete stranger." I huffed. "You know, *some* gay men are dangerous."

"Get back to bed," Detective Downey told us. "We'll be stopping by again in the morning."

"I'm afraid we're out of pağaças," I said.

Demir gave me a side eye. But he and Detective Downey walked back out the front door. I locked it, locked the back door, and joined Tommy again in the living room. He hadn't moved.

"They're going to pin this on me," he said. "It won't matter if the police planted evidence or if the murderer did. Either way, no one's going to question whether a jealous savage killed these men."

"I know you didn't do it," I said.

He gave me a long, cold look. "Do you?" he asked. "I didn't know you had a gun."

There was nothing to be gained by going over that right now. If Tommy had been jealous or angry with me, he could have killed *me*, not some random strangers I hadn't even had sex with. He was my beneficiary, after all. Even if he'd been planning to plant the supposed evidence on me at some point, he had nothing to gain from my imprisonment.

Unless he just wanted me to be miserable. Of course, if that was his goal, all he had to do was turn on the news a few minutes longer every day.

"Sometimes," Tommy said, "I think all white people are the enemy. Even the ones who think they're allies."

My mouth fell open.

Simply because Tommy was from a more marginalized group than I was didn't mean that his views and moral judgements on everything were always "right." Lots of people in every marginalized group had plenty of questionable opinions. Just as I wouldn't vote for a candidate simply because he was an "out, proud gay man," I also didn't accept that those who had suffered more systemic oppression than I had always got to tell me what to do or feel. Sometimes, Tommy was right, and sometimes, he wasn't. Sometimes, neither of us was.

Moral ambiguity sucked.

I understood the desire of many on the far right to be told what to think. But Tommy and I weren't able to live that way. We had to muddle through on our own.

"Kind of like when your family pouts," Tommy added, "and says in that sweet, sad tone, 'We'll put your name on the temple prayer roll.'"

God damn. LDS leaders had long instructed members to date and marry within their race and class. It had always seemed to me a way of propagating hierarchies. But there was clearly some practical use to it. Our cultural differences did add difficulty, even in the best of times. And these were not the best.

But then, every relationship had its problems, and my marriage to Tommy was by far my most successful.

Until it wasn't?

I looked at him, his face still expressionless.

I walked over to my husband, stood in front of him a moment, and took his hands in mine. "I will find who did this," I said, "even if it kills me."

Tommy sighed.

"Let's get back to bed." I led him to the bedroom and crawled in beside him, making myself the bigger spoon, and hugged him until daylight. Neither of us spoke, but I could tell from his breathing that neither of us slept, either.

Chapter Sixteen

Sunday morning. The Ethiopian Christians across the street started arriving around 4:30 and kept streaming in for the next hour. They'd be there for another six. Even Mormons weren't that dedicated.

Though I did remember the Keatons. When I was a kid, the family had bought a home directly across the street from our ward, which also functioned as the stake center. The father said he wanted to be ready to accept any leadership position the Lord called him to. His family would never be late for meetings. They could always pitch in to help at the last minute. One of the five children was Scott, a boy my age. He told me they dressed in their Sunday best for dinner every night of the week, a nice dress for the girls and a suit and tie for the boys. They didn't own a television. The family was held up as a shining example for the ward, but I always knew I never wanted to live that way.

I could hear Connie Francis singing, "Who's Sorry Now?"

Not me, I realized, a bit surprised. Despite everything, I wouldn't go back. And even if the new administration came after every single LGBTQ person in the country next year, I still wouldn't.

I remembered my brother Jared telling me, "On Judgment Day, every knee shall bow and every tongue confess. You'll know you made the wrong choice and you'll be forced to accept the gospel then. But it'll be too late."

Even *if* that were the truth, even that wouldn't change my mind. People might obey Orbán or Putin out of fear, but they didn't do it out of love or because it was right. With that kind of God, even heaven would be hell.

I'd already accepted the truth about myself. And I'd chosen Tommy.

"Are you ready?" he whispered.

This day was likely to be the worst of my life.

"Turn over," he said softly.

We'd been spooning the past few hours. I expected now to be the little spoon for a while, but he gently pushed until I was lying face down.

I heard him fumbling with something in the nightstand. I felt a slight rush of adrenalin, surprised my body could still produce any.

And then I felt something wet on my asshole. "We may not get many more chances to do this," he said.

Tommy entered me slowly and began gently thrusting, but before long, he was pounding away as if trying to break through drywall. Usually, any pain while being fucked took place in the first minute or so. This morning, though, the pain kept increasing as he pounded harder and harder.

Twice in two days. A rags to riches story.

"We can't always choose what happens to us in this life," Elder Sass, one of my favorite companions, had told me one day, "but we can choose how we react." With a name like that, I hoped he'd turned out gay, but I'd lost contact with him after our missionary days and had no idea.

Tommy's groan when he came was almost a scream. Then he collapsed on top of me, his chest sticky with sweat, with more sweat dripping onto the back of my neck.

"Sorry," he mumbled.

"It's okay," I told him. I'd learned long ago not to say, "I understand." I really couldn't, anyway, and those words could be triggering.

"I wish…" he said. "I wish…"

"I know."

"Let's get cleaned up," Tommy said. "The police could be back any minute."

We took turns showering, ate a couple of protein waffles with sugar-free jam, and tried to straighten up some of the mess left over after the rushed search overnight. The place hadn't been ransacked, but the officers hadn't been gentle, either. Gathering up a box of spilled cotton swabs and fluticasone bottles, I felt my jaw clenching.

Someone had done this to us.

I was easily irritated but rarely angry. I'd only once ever felt a murderous rage, over four decades earlier. My first missionary companion in Rome had pushed me to recite lesson H before I'd fully memorized it. We needed to "pass off" each lesson before we could prove we were ready to become senior companions. I was in no rush. After all, most juniors had several seniors before advancing. But my average progress was a reflection on *him* and therefore unacceptable.

It had taken me over three hours to recite the forty-five minute lesson because I kept pausing so often and backtracking. When I finally stumbled over the finish line, Elder Ramsay had said, with a sneer so triggering I still felt sick whenever I heard anyone else use the tone, "Do you really think that was good enough? You'll need to do it again." He'd dismissed me with a wave of his hand and walked away to stand on our balcony. I'd had to head for the bathroom to keep myself from pushing him over the railing and going straight to hell.

But I wanted to kill whoever had done this to Tommy and me. And to Salvador and Peter. This was someone who shouldn't be here any longer.

Unfortunately, while there might not be a hell, there were private prisons, and I didn't want to go there, either.

"What if it was Clayton?" I asked suddenly.

"Huh?"

All this time, I'd been assuming it was one of the regulars at the club, but Clayton had left before the murder was discovered, too. Would he have had time to plant evidence? Could the murderer in fact be working with a partner?

"There are *so* many suspects," I moaned. "How will the police ever figure out who did this?"

I realized it was the wrong thing to say as soon as the words were out of my mouth. Why was talking to someone you loved so difficult? Trying to recover, I started on a tangent, hoping to distract Tommy. "Let's have a Companion Inventory," I said.

To his credit, Tommy managed not to groan. "Do you have a problem with me?" he asked dryly.

"MAGA cultists are cruel," I said.

He blinked. "Are we debating?"

"They're *addicted* to their cruelty."

Tommy pressed his lips. "Are you supposed to be saying something profound?"

I shrugged. "People with addictions of any kind need stronger and stronger doses to get their high." We were in for some rough times over the coming months under the new administration, would probably face some life and death circumstances, and it felt astonishingly unfair that we might lose our freedom *today*, over a month before they even took office.

Tommy had never taken so much as a sip of alcohol, first warned away from it by the LDS church and then intimidated by the rate of alcoholism in some native communities. We could be influenced by stereotypes as much as anyone else.

"People in oppressed groups can be cruel, too," I said. Salvador had proven that. As had those who treated Marin so badly.

But Clayton? Jelani? Tuyen?

Who had done this? Who in our circle had been so cruel to at least four of us now?

"Jack off clubs are supposed to be fun," I said. "Casual sex is supposed to be fun. Sex with friends. Sex with..." I almost said "husbands" but stopped myself.

And it wasn't just gay men who could be cruel to other gay men. A week or so ago, I'd seen a local news story about a brutal membership battle within the Squaxin tribe, another group here in the Pacific Northwest.

They'd recently removed the names of dozens of members, people in their fifties and sixties who'd spent their entire lives as tribal members, whose parents and grandparents had been Squaxin as well, simply because these now excommunicated members couldn't provide the proper paperwork to prove something that had happened before they were even born.

"If it comes down to it," I said, "I'll confess. I won't let them destroy you."

Tommy looked at me, his face expressionless.

How awful that he'd needed to learn how to do that.

"A white savior to the rescue," he said so softly I almost couldn't hear him.

I took a deep breath. "Let's go on a date. Right now."

"Aren't the detectives due back soon?"

Probably. There was no way to contact them without our phones or computers, no way for them to contact us, either. "We'll leave a note telling them where we are."

"And where will we be?"

"Capitol Hill," I said, forcing a smile. "If they wanted to track us, they should have let us keep our phones." I shrugged again. "And if they'd wanted to arrest either of us, they'd have done it last night. They didn't say we *couldn't* leave the house." Maybe they didn't really suspect Tommy. Maybe they were just going through the motions because they were required to follow every tip.

Since Demir had looked up my history online, I knew he could have done the same for Tommy. Seen that Tommy volunteered regularly at a food bank in the Central District, that he used to donate plasma twice a month at Harborview until he was forbidden once the clinic learned he was gay. Seen that for the past decade he volunteered to teach a Watercolor Dementia class a few times each year.

Demir would have seen that Tommy was even listed as an associate producer on a documentary about polyamory among indigenous populations. He wasn't someone who would kill because his husband was going to a sex club.

I jotted a quick note and placed it on the coffee table. I couldn't very well tape it to the front door announcing, "No one's home but we'll be back in a few hours."

Would someone try to plant additional evidence if we left the house? It was impossible to know. But we couldn't live in constant fear.

Actually, I *did* often live in fear. How could we not as we watched fascism approaching like a dust storm across the plains? What we couldn't do, though, was let it paralyze us.

"We'll leave the door unlocked," I said, "so the police don't break it down if we don't answer." Tommy shook his head in an I-can't-believe-I'm-going-along-with-this look. "Let's go."

I grabbed my keys and Orca pass and gave Tommy a kiss. When we opened the door to head out, Detectives Downey and Altan were on the porch. Demir had his hand raised to knock.

Chapter Seventeen

I waved the detectives inside. They hadn't asked permission, and I suppose I could have kept them on the porch and spoken through the open door or the speakeasy window, but there didn't seem to be any point after all they'd already taken from us.

"Thank you," Detective Downey said. Her hair was in a short bob today. How did she manage to style it so differently so often? I wore the same boring hair day after day. I needed to dye it blue or green or purple. Live a little.

Detective Altan gave a small nod in my direction, just enough to signal something beyond a professional encounter. I was surprised how moved I felt by the tiny gesture.

The officers sat on the sofa while Tommy took the armchair and I pulled out the ottoman. It struck me that ottomans must have originated in the Ottoman Empire.

"We did find the layout of the sex club on your computer, Mr. Tahoma," Detective Downey began. "But so far nothing else suspicious."

"And our digital forensics team can see the map was downloaded a week and a half ago," Demir said. "*After* the first murder."

"It doesn't prove anything one way or the other," Detective Downey continued, "but the timing is less suspicious, not more."

"I didn't download it at all," Tommy said. "Did someone break in here twice?" He looked at me, his brows furrowed.

"First thing Monday, we're making an appointment to have a security system installed." I was too far from Tommy to squeeze his hand but gave him a nod, hoping he found it as encouraging as I'd felt when Demir did it.

"When do we get our phones and computers back?" Tommy asked, his tone cool rather than neutral.

"I'd like to say later today," Detective Downey replied, "but it's Sunday. Better to expect your devices tomorrow."

Tommy gave a half shrug, not looking at the detectives.

"We have just a few additional questions while we're here," Demir said. He pulled up a photo on his phone and showed me. The image was of an elderly man I'd seen many times at the club.

"I don't know his name," I said. He'd been there for the questioning the day before, but I hadn't paid attention when he'd given his name. It was the other answers I hoped would be more revealing.

"What are your thoughts about the guy?" Demir continued.

"He catches your eye from ten or fifteen feet away," I said. "Then he approaches, looking interested, but when he gets close enough, he changes his mind and walks away."

"He did that to you?"

I laughed. "He's done it several times. Does it to others, too. That's what he gets off on. Now that I know this is his 'thing,' I go along, try to look excited and then disappointed."

Demir coughed.

"Whatever floats his boat," I said.

Detective Downey focused her gaze on me a long moment, gave her partner a dismissive glance, and turned back to me again. She showed me two more photographs. The first was another regular I had little to say about. The other was a newbie I hadn't interacted with the day before. I'd seen him goose a couple of guys, which was against the rules. I'd then seen Clayton whisper something to him. And then the guy had stuck to the rules the rest of the time. At least as far as I knew. I rarely watched any one man for very long while at the club. There was a smorgasbord of men to appreciate.

"Do you actually suspect any of these guys?" I asked.

"Just following up on some information," Detective Downey said. She stood up to leave, so the rest of us stood as well. Demir asked to use the bathroom first, so everyone else stood around awkwardly while we listened to him piss like a racehorse another couple of moments before they headed out.

After the detectives left, I turned to Tommy. "Part of me wants to huddle under a blanket the rest of the day and nap, but if you're up for that outing to Capitol Hill, let's do it."

"I'll make some sandwiches, and we can eat lunch in Volunteer Park." A bit cold, but we might not have the chance in April.

Light rail was down. One of the trains had hit a car. So we caught the 106 to Mount Baker and then transferred to the 8. It wasn't until we sat down that I noticed a well-dressed Asian man in the Disability section, wearing a purple suit and pink tie, with a conical bamboo sun hat, hardly necessary given the clouds and chilly mist this morning. He also carried a pistol in each hand.

They looked like water pistols, made of orange, green, and white plastic. It wasn't clear if the liquid in the transparent chambers was water or bleach or something else.

Not a bad idea, really. Everyone steered clear of the guy. Even a mugger would likely choose another target. Tommy and I still needed to talk about the weapon I'd hidden in my office, but if things got bad in the coming months under the new administration, a good first step might be to start carrying loaded water pistols. Of course, giving out *I'm crazy* vibes could go either way. Would they be enough to keep the initial round of bad guys away without being so provocative they'd draw the attention of the police?

Tommy and I walked along both sides of Broadway, stopping in a thrift store, where I managed not to buy anything, and then appreciating the LGBTQ-friendly signage in various shop windows. "Safe Space" in rainbow colors.

"No Hate Here" in rainbow colors. "Banking that serves YOUR needs" featuring a gay couple and a lesbian couple.

Despite those happy messages, I struggled to suppress my inner Get-Off-My-Lawn as young folks bumped into us, unable to keep their eyes off their cell phones. And while I had a take it or leave it attitude toward fresh piss, the smell of ammonia from some of the doorways and bus shelters did little for me.

As we paused on the corner of East John, I pointed to an apartment window across the street, three floors up. Someone had placed a New York license plate against the glass. It read "ASSMAN."

Now *that* was a welcoming sign.

"Oh!"

I stumbled into the street just as the 49 came barreling forward. Tommy grabbed my jacket and yanked me back seconds before the bus passed. A man on one side of us grunted in concern while at least two women gasped.

"You okay?" Tommy asked, his face inches from mine, his eyes searching.

"Someone pushed me."

Was I Doris fucking Day? I was growing familiar with the sensation of adrenalin flowing through my body. Broadway in Seattle wasn't like Broadway in New York. Even our thickest crowds were relatively light. But this was a major intersection. The busiest entrance to the Capitol Hill light rail station was on this corner, plus two buses stopped on Broadway and three others on John.

I looked behind me now, hoping to recognize anyone walking away, but there was no one with a familiar stride, no one whose ass I recognized, nothing.

The light changed and the others waiting near us crossed the street, whatever concern they'd felt over the near miss already dissipated. No homeless folks among that crowd. Capitol Hill had seen a large influx of tech bros over the past few years, though, and a couple of months ago, a group of young men had shouted slurs outside a gay bar.

That shove could have come from any of those young, clean-cut men who'd just crossed the street. If it had been an accident, someone would have apologized.

I couldn't help but remember that I'd been slightly ahead and to the side of Tommy at the curb. That shove *could* have come from him.

No. I wasn't going there. This was what the bad guys wanted. Suspicion and division. I grabbed Tommy's hand. "Let's go to the park."

As we reached East Republican, we bumped into Nathan and a friend of his I'd heard him talk about but who I'd never met. They'd gotten together for a late morning blow job and were now on their way to have lunch and see a matinee.

Volunteer Park, at the north end of Capitol Hill, was a small but glorious public space. At least a dozen sequoias throughout the park soared majestically into the sky, but there were also lovely cedars, pines, and firs, as well as an Asian Art Museum and a Conservatory filled with exotic plants. And this time of year, the moss on tree branches and steps and walls shone vibrantly green.

I could see a ship out on the Sound heading north toward the strait.

The mist had melted away, but the benches were still damp. Tommy pointed toward the brick water tower, and we headed inside, climbing a hundred steps to the top. There were a few others admiring the view, but it was still early, not quite noon, and Seattleites usually got a late start on weekends.

Tommy handed me a sandwich and took one for himself. We stood looking through the barred window at the expensive mansions below and ate quietly. Even after we both finished, we continued to stand in silence. Tommy took my hand as we looked out over the city below.

"I can't believe," I finally said, "how *tired* I feel."

"What do you want to do?"

I wasn't sure. "I want to quit," I said. "And I want to fight back." I could already see media moguls giving in ahead of time to the new administration, could see Democratic politicians moving to the right instead of pushing stronger to the left.

I didn't like being a target. I wanted to leave the jack off murderer alone so he'd leave me alone.

But I also wanted to nail him and make him pay.

"I think," I said, "that—"

My phone vibrated and I checked the screen. Chris was calling. I still felt a bit miffed over his comment during questioning, but there weren't many other people I could talk to about this ongoing trauma, so I motioned to Tommy, shrugged, and answered.

"Hey, Bruce, how are you?"

"Dandy." I put the phone on Speaker.

Tommy turned away and looked back toward the mansions below.

"Good, good. Have you heard any more developments? Did that detective tell you anything the rest of us don't know?"

I debated how to answer. I needed Chris's PI skills, but I didn't have anything concrete to follow up on. While I was greatly enjoying the renewed intimacy with Tommy, I also missed the casual friendliness of encounters with Chris. No matter how much I liked a five-layer lasagna, there'd always be times a quick sandwich would hit the spot better. With Tommy, it sometimes felt like I got both at the same time. But only sometimes.

There had to be times when Chris and I only connected as friends and not fuck buddies for the "buddy" part to feel real.

"They received an anonymous tip," I said carefully, "and it seems to be leading them in the right direction." Tommy turned back toward me, one eyebrow raised.

"Really?"

"They didn't want to tell me any more than that."

Tommy scoffed.

"So you don't have any clue what the tip was?" Chris pressed.

"Nope."

There was a pause. "Are you mad about something, Bruce? You seem a little curt."

Now it was my turn to pause. "What was all that 'Bruce isn't shady but maybe he is' crap about yesterday?"

I could hear Chris sighing heavily into the phone. "I'm sorry," he said. "I couldn't catch myself in time. I'd talked to this Peter guy a few minutes during the event. He pointed you out, said he knew you, and I told him we were investigating a murder together."

"You told him there was a murder at the club?"

"He had a right to know. Especially considering that he was *obviously* in danger."

True, but Chris hadn't known that.

"The guy acted put out *you* hadn't said anything to him."

Shit. What if I'd urged him to leave and come back at another time instead of doing nothing?

"I didn't want to say all that to the detectives," Chris went on. "Not in front of everyone."

Something about his phrasing caught my attention. "And did you tell them while *not* in front of everyone?"

"No, no."

There was another long moment of silence. Tommy was studying me, his eyes narrowed.

"Are we okay now, Bruce?"

"Have *you* learned anything new since yesterday?" I asked.

"I went to see Marin again last night at his place. Can I come over soon so we can talk in person?"

Chris hadn't actually apologized. Explaining the reasons for poor behavior wasn't exactly the same thing. But it did seem innocent enough. I supposed. If I was grading on a curve.

I didn't really know the guy that well. It could be he was just a bit of a jerk and liked drama. There were plenty of gay men like that. If there was ever a time to cut someone some slack, it was at times like this. While Demir had told me not to meet up with anyone from the club until further notice, I really didn't believe Chris was the killer.

When things were dire, though, everyone suspected everyone else. It was what made MAGA successful. Poor Latinos were after the jobs of poor white folks. If your kids weren't doing well in school, it wasn't because schools were underfunded. It was because trans people taught student furries to use litter boxes. We were afraid to call out genocide in Gaza because we'd be labeled antisemitic, which would undermine our core sense of solidarity with a different oppressed group.

Everyone's motives were questioned, everyone was accused of one moral slip or another. Enemies attacked us and allies called us out. We had to worry about every single person we interacted with.

Divide and conquer. Divide and conquer. Divide and conquer.

We were all losers if we didn't stick together.

Still, I was exhausted. And I wanted to dedicate more time to Tommy. Either one of us could still end up arrested before this was over. Or dead.

"Maybe this Friday," I said. "Tommy's been fucking me again, and he's got a big dick. I'm pretty sore."

Tommy's lip twitched.

"You could always just suck my dick." Chris laughed.

"Why don't we Zoom tomorrow night and go over everything we know again?" I suggested.

"Okay, okay. But only if we talk with our shirts off."

The following Wednesday was Christmas, and the week after that New Year's Eve. Tommy and I might be separated before Wednesday, and if we weren't, it might be our last Christmas together, depending on how quickly Project 2025 was enacted. So much to think about, so much to do, but the only thing I wanted to do right now was go home.

No ruby slippers to click together.

"Tommy," I said, "how do you feel about napping on the sofa with me and then playing a game of Scrabble?"

He nodded. "Then can we order some Greek food?"

"We'll even have them deliver some baklava."

Chapter Eighteen

I dozed on the sofa sitting up. Tommy lay his head in my lap, and I put my hand on his chest while he napped.

I'd say the Scrabble game later went as usual, but really, it was never routine. Tommy always managed to both surprise and delight me with the words he put on the board. He turned my "hog" to "hogan" and my "quest" to "request." *He* was the one who ended up with the double word score using that Q. Even when I managed to turn his "comb" to "combat," he followed up by turning the word into "combative" on the next round. We quickly ran out of space on the board, but Tommy still managed to add a D or S or R to words ending in E.

We streamed the French movie *Auction* while eating our Greek dinner. In the film, a man discovers he's inherited a multi-million dollar painting that was stolen from Jews during the Holocaust. The masterpiece had been purchased sometime after 1939, perhaps unknowingly, by his family. When the surviving legitimate heirs offer to pay for the returned painting, the man refuses. "I don't want blood money."

I needed a feel good movie tonight.

If you could ever call the awful aftermath of a genocide "feel good."

"Tommy," I said when the film was over, "want to watch a couple of self-defense videos?" It was an odd use of quality time, but these were skills we needed, if one of us was going to be in prison. Or even if we were both living "free" under this new administration.

"Are we butch enough to fend off a mugger?" he asked with a tiny smile.

"These videos are designed to teach little old ladies," I returned with my own smile.

"Oh, snap!"

Whether we were too old for self-defense, we were certainly too old for slang like that. We headed for my office, where I suddenly realized we still didn't have our devices back. I huffed. "We *are* old. We're both losing our memory at the same time." I supposed we could probably have watched YouTube on the television, but neither of us was up to figuring out how to do that just now.

Instead, I went over a couple of easy moves with Tommy. We practiced not backing away when someone lunged forward but instead grabbing their shirt and pulling them even closer while lowering our head and smashing their face into the thickest part of our skull. Then we practiced throat punches. "And don't stop to evaluate the damage," I said. "Either run or keep attacking until they can't move."

"Jesus Christ, Bruce. Is this supposed to convince me you're not a murderer?"

Tommy wasn't looking any more polished than I was, so it didn't appear that *he* was the murderer, either.

We might both need to become killers at some point, though, if we wanted to survive the next few years. Of course, that did beg the question. Did we *want* to survive the next few years if we needed to become so brutal?

I felt like the experimental subject in a room filling with smoke. In the instructional film I'd watched in college, the subjects see the smoke, but they don't realize the other people in the room are part of the experiment. When those others don't react, the subject looks confused. Is this not really a problem? Should she say something? Will he look stupid if he does? As the smoke thickens, he looks more conflicted. Why didn't anyone else see what she was seeing?

Most of the subjects eventually acted, but a couple waited until the room was almost completely unnavigable.

Every time I listened to a news anchor or pundit question whether the horrible promises from the new administration were dangerous, I saw smoke. And when the anchors pooh-poohed it, I worried I was overreacting.

And every day, the smoke grew thicker.

I wanted to call in sick the next day, spend Monday with Tommy, have him call in sick, too. Without phones, though, we'd have to knock on a neighbor's door and ask to use theirs. And who wanted to answer the obvious question,

"What happened to *your* phones?" It seemed unlikely that everyone in the neighborhood had slept through the police visit. There'd been no sirens or flashing lights, so we might have lucked out. But I didn't want to find out.

"Tommy," I said, "you staying home tomorrow so you can be here when the police bring our devices back? I can call your job when I get to work and tell them you're sick."

"I'm not sure I want to be alone with the police."

"Oh."

"Why don't I go to work and call *your* supervisor?"

So that's what we did. Detective Altan looked fit and well rested when I opened the door. Detective Downey's blue braids were back. Demir offered to help me reconnect the computers, but I declined. It was difficult not to suspect they'd placed some kind of monitoring device in them, but really, what would have been the point? If there wasn't any evidence on our computers already, we'd hardly go out of our way to put anything incriminating on them now, especially if we were guilty. And knowing we were still suspects, we'd probably not even look up anything that could remotely be misconstrued as problematic.

Apparently, my browser history of self-defense videos hadn't set off any alarms. Unless the detectives were keeping mum while still building their case.

What did it say about me that I was also thinking about anything a fascist regime might find on my computer if someone came looking? Residency permits for Italy. Living off the grid for a week. Best places to hide money in your home. I wondered if worry was more exhausting than fear. I needed to find a way to move beyond it.

Demir lingered behind after his partner headed back to their car. The day was cool but clear, no clouds for a change. Detective Downey leaned against the car, her face turned up toward the sun, her eyes closed, a tiny smile on her face.

"I need to use your restroom," Demir said.

I nodded as he headed deeper into the house. When he reached the bathroom door, he nodded back, jerking his head in invitation.

Really?

But I followed, standing in the doorway as he unzipped and aimed. I remembered my missionary days, when I lived in groups of four or six young men sharing a single bathroom. Someone was always naked in the morning. And someone always came into the bathroom to brush their teeth or start a load of laundry while someone else was peeing.

We'd been taught to sing a hymn when we needed help keeping our thoughts pure, but my mind had returned time and again to, "Ye elders of Israel, come join now with me," and "joining" would bring up all sorts of images in my brain. Not helpful.

"I'll be honest with you, Bruce," Demir said, his stream hitting the water. "We have no idea who's behind these murders."

"I'd say I wish I could help, but…"

"You're not sleuthing anymore?"

I shrugged. "It only feels like sleuthing if I ask the right person the right question, and I don't seem to have done that. So I don't know what the hell I've been doing."

He laughed and shook his penis before turning to me and zipping up.

"Is this another test to see how casual I can be in provocative situations?"

He laughed again. "Sounds like you asked at least one good question to the right person," he observed.

I had to admit, I liked how weird the man was. It wasn't easy finding other people whose weirdness fit so well with my own. "I really do hope you'll come over for dinner when this is all over."

"Now that I've studied your browser history," he said, "I'll definitely take you up on it." He passed me in the doorway, brushing against me, and headed for the front door. Just before he opened it, he turned around. "I had to look up Abdi Nazemian," he said. "But I'll want to borrow that book when you're done with it."

After he left, I sat on the sofa and finished the last few chapters of *Dying of Curiosity*. Then I streamed a movie on Kanopy, *Agatha and the Truth of Murder*, an alternate history version of what could have happened during the eleven days

Agatha Christie went missing. The conclusion was almost laugh out loud funny. Ingenious.

The least likely suspect? The most likely?

I went over the jack off club killings again and again. What was I missing? The answer *had* to already be there. We couldn't all have missed it.

I cut some blackberry vines in the yard, easy to do during the winter when they grew at a slightly slower pace. I walked to the grocery and bought a piece of high fiber chocolate cake for Tommy. God only knew how it was going to taste. And I took a shower, spreading my cheeks afterward and then exposing my balls to a box fan to keep from developing jock itch.

That kind of thing was a complete turn off for Tommy, but I couldn't help wondering if Demir would take it all in stride. I also couldn't help but wonder if Tommy might be open to taking turns dating Demir.

Or if Demir would be open to it, either. There seemed a real value to having different people to share different parts of your personality with. Not just casually, as I did with Nathan, but in a more committed manner.

All ideas to be explored later. Under the new authoritarian regime.

No one ever accused me of having good timing.

Late in the afternoon, I heard my phone ping. A text. Probably Chris checking in to see if I'd learned anything. I also needed to ask if he had. But it turned out to be Clayton.

"We need an extra play date to make up for the disasters," he wrote.

Noting the euphemism, I texted back. "Need a volunteer?"

"How about tomorrow? Christmas Eve. We'll have a theme night. Sitting on Santa's Lap."

Damn. Time had really escaped me. Too much going on.

Tommy and I usually watched *A Christmas Story* each year on Christmas Eve. A couple of years ago, we'd added *Anna and the Apocalypse* to make it a double feature. We saved *Last Holiday* for Christmas Day. And we always took a long walk, no matter the weather.

I wouldn't have to worry about the murderer. Tommy would kill me himself if I went to the event.

"Let me ask my husband when he gets home," I texted back.

"Thx."

I had dinner on the table five minutes after Tommy walked through the door. "Fried egg sandwiches and hash browns?" he asked. "Did you catch an STI?"

"I can serve comfort food just to be nice." He gave me a look, and I explained what Clayton had suggested. "Even if you weren't opposed to it," I said, "I don't know that I could go through all that again. Not even if everything went smoothly."

Tommy took a bite of his sandwich while the egg was still steaming. "But it's obvious you do want to or you wouldn't have mentioned it at all."

I laughed. "Why don't *you* go to PI school?"

He swallowed and stared at me. "We could go together," he said slowly. "Have a buddy system. Never let each other out of our sight."

Oh my god. Did it take two murders for us to finally have a sexual adventure together? I texted Clayton and told him Tommy would help with the set-up, too. He replied that he'd hired five security guards, paying them out of his own pocket, to make sure we had at least one successful event before the club collapsed forever.

After dinner, I texted Demir and invited him to join the group as well. "It's not illegal to have fun on your time off," I pointed out when he called back. I put the phone on Speaker.

"You just want to see my dick," he said.

"I've already seen it," I reminded him.

Tommy gave me a look.

"It won't hurt to have an officer on the scene in addition to the security guards," I said. "And if the guys start seeing you as 'one of us,' they might be more willing to answer questions." It wasn't as if he didn't already have a conflict of interest.

"You've convinced me," he said, a bit too quickly, I thought.

"You just want to see *my* dick," I joked.

"I want to see *Tommy's* dick," he replied.

Tommy gave me another look, this one with a raised eyebrow. "I think that can be arranged," I said. "In fact, since we'll all be naked, I think it's inevitable."

"See you tomorrow night."

I hung up and turned to Tommy. "Merry Christmas," he said.

I washed dishes while he ate his cake, and then we settled in for an episode of *Hjerson*, a Swedish adaptation of Agatha Christie stories. In this series, one of the lead characters was openly gay. And occasionally nude.

I loved European programming.

Chapter Nineteen

Tuesday morning, Demir sent me a text with a photo of his bathroom. Clean and inviting. His toilet even had a bidet feature.

Since I usually tried to meet up with Nathan on Tuesday evenings after work, I called during my lunch break to explain the change of plans. I found myself more disappointed than he seemed to be, realizing that the intimacy of a single sexual friendship, even if our encounters weren't always sexual, was far more rewarding than a roomful of naked men. Of course, it wasn't usually an either/or decision to make, but I worried I was making the wrong one this time.

"I'm going with a few of my Jewish friends to an anti-genocide rally tomorrow," Nathan said.

"Can non-Jews come?" I asked. It was raining moderately now but was supposed to clear up in the morning.

"I've got an extra kippah." He paused. "I mean, it's not a costume," he added, "but it is. The whole thing feels a bit self-righteous. We'll be posting pictures online with our signs in front of the Federal building. Even though no one's going to be in the Federal building on Christmas. We're just being performative."

Of course tomorrow's protest was performative. Every protest was. "Don't let anyone shame you into being silent," I said. "Just make sure you contact lots of media so at least someone covers it. Don't count on someone else to do it."

I kept a list of News Tip emails and phone numbers in a Word doc, plus the emails of a handful of specific reporters who covered "leftist" topics positively, just as I kept phone numbers for the governor and my state legislator on my cell phone. Over the past few months, I'd also begun calling my senators and state representative almost every time I found myself waiting for the bus. Two or three sentences on a given topic was all it took. I felt nervous and uncomfortable every single time, and it wasn't clear it ever made the slightest difference, but it was something I could do, so I did it.

I should have started calling years ago.

I texted Greg, the guy who lived out in SeaTac, asking if he'd like to come over on Saturday to watch a movie.

Only moments after returning to my cashier post when my lunch break was over, I received a text. Thinking it might be Greg replying, I stole a quick glance, only to see it was an alert that the city council was holding a previously unscheduled meeting in two hours—on Christmas Eve!—trying to repeal an ethics rule preventing council members from voting on issues when there was a conflict of interest. The landlords on the council wanted to repeal that rule so they could then repeal a host of renters' rights that had passed under the last council's tenure.

The barrage of attacks from every direction was relentless. And these were all Democrats.

I was surprised there weren't more sex clubs popping up across the city. We all needed to relieve stress pretty much all the time.

I shot a quick text to several friends, asking them to send in public comments.

The courts closed an hour earlier today. I was home before Tommy and hopped in the shower. Then I had veggie burgers on keto bread, with a small serving of sweet potato fries and a small dill pickle, ready when Tommy walked through the door. We washed it down with coconut lime kombucha.

We both popped a dick pill before heading for light rail.

"Damn," I said, pulling my hood tight as we waited for the train to pull up. "Awful late for a windstorm." We usually had two or three of them each November.

"What's our plan if the lights go out at the club?"

"Clayton will have some flashlights or battery-operated lamps ready."

"Are you sure?" Tommy asked. "Or just hoping?"

Given the temptation to do more than jack off at the club, I felt confident Clayton would not want everyone in the dark for long.

A thin, black man of indeterminate age—somewhere between thirty and fifty—sat hunched on a covered bench at the light rail station, but the shelter was no match for the biting wind. He wrapped himself in a thin blanket, leaving only part of his forehead peeking through, and leaned against the cracked glass partition. A few homeless folks slept in the rear seats of most light rail cars, spending the day bouncing back and forth between Angle Lake and Lynnwood. This guy looked like he wanted to sit still for a while instead.

I felt for him. But at the same time, I wanted him to go away. I didn't want to see him. Or the hundreds like him I passed every day almost everywhere I went in the city. I understood the impulse to hide "them" away.

I wanted relief from *everyone's* misery.

But hiding from reality wasn't the same as solving a problem.

The thought tickled the back of my brain. Was it something Chris had said? Demir?

Something about misdirection.

The wind whipped the man's blanket away from his face. He scrunched his nose and lowered himself to the pavement, wedging himself in the corner beside the bench, and pulled the blanket back over his head.

Usually, while I rode up to Jack Off Buddies, I looked at the other riders, wondering what they'd think if they knew my destination. This evening, though, I wondered what *they* were all up to. That shrunken old Asian man with a shopping bag, his head nodding sleepily, looked suspiciously like one of the club's regulars.

We met Demir half a block from the club's entrance and walked over together after the doors opened. I had free entry because of my previous volunteering, but Tommy and Demir both had to pay $20. They'd both also had to go online earlier and sign up for a membership. "And now we wait under the boobs with the tassles," I said, pointing to a row of chairs in the foyer.

The boobs in question were papier-mâché breasts glued to a portrait within a gilded frame, with what looked like silk curtain cords attached to the nipples. They protruded four inches from the canvas. "This is where the new members wait to be taken to orientation," I added.

We usually had eight to ten new members at each event, but tonight only two other men joined us. The late addition of the play date, along with holiday commitments, was likely the reason.

That or the murder rate.

Because Tommy, Demir, and I had committed to stick together the entire evening, I joined them in the locker room for New Member Orientation. Since I might volunteer to be the "teacher" at some point, it didn't hurt to hear a refresher.

"The main thing to remember," the man concluded, "is that you can jack yourself off, you can jack a buddy off, or you can have a buddy jack you off. But nothing goes in anyone's anything."

I remembered Pee Wee Herman's career being destroyed when he was arrested in an adult movie theater.

I also remembered watching the movie *Radium Girls*, about the young women who ingested radioactive paint while working on watches and clocks in the early twentieth century. When they realized why they were developing cancer and dying, they sought justice. But their employer had the perfect way to discredit their claims.

The young women were ill because they were tramps and had caught a "venereal disease."

No one listened to the women after that.

When the new administration came after LGBTQ folks, who would listen to us once we were labeled sex freaks? Even in my attempt to overcome my religious background and become sex positive, I still recognized that the innocuous act of masturbation made me a pervert in the eyes of many.

I could envision a day under Project 2025 when all LGBTQ folks were legally marked as sex offenders, simply for existing, even if they were celibate virgins.

Would those laws be passed during Pride month next year?

Why couldn't the Jack Off Club killer go after the bad guys?

You're here tonight to have fun, I reminded myself. *Have fun!*

By the time we finished orientation and grabbed our padlocks, we couldn't find lockers next to each other, but the changing area was small, so we were never more than a few feet apart. Demir and I both looked down where we'd seen Sal, but I didn't point out the spot to Tommy.

Soon, we were naked except for our shoes, standing roughly in a circle, staring at one another. I'd already seen Demir's dick, but Tommy hadn't. It was fun to watch him look. I rather enjoyed seeing Demir survey both of us as well.

I reached over and touched Tommy's dick gently. "Shall we go find some admirers?" I asked.

He smiled, Demir licked a fingertip and touched his right nipple, and we headed up the stairs together. I made Demir go first.

It wasn't until I pulled on a green wrist band upstairs that I realized I'd forgotten to remove my Do Not Resuscitate necklace. I didn't want to lead everyone back downstairs, so I turned the message toward my skin and directed us to sit near the massage table. Always lots of action in this section of the play space, with a clear view of the video screen, too.

One of the regulars, a bear of a black man, sat in a large chair against the wall in the middle of the room. He wore a Santa cap, black boots, and a red jock strap with a white fur border. Guys took turns sitting in his lap.

Clayton offered to take pictures with his cell phone, the only phone allowed on the floor tonight, for those who wanted one.

The security guards reminded me of the Swiss guards I'd seen at the Vatican, silent, unmoving, but alert.

The music was loud, but we could have talked over it if we'd wanted to. Neither Tommy nor Demir seemed so inclined, both trying to take in as much of their surroundings as possible. It was fun watching their eyes flit in every direction, suggesting excitement despite their blank faces.

Men were great at hiding their thoughts.

It was possibly one of the reasons I wasn't as successful here as some of the other men. I smiled a lot in this space. Most of the others revealed no emotion at all. Smiling wasn't butch.

Perhaps Marin had gotten the memo. He was here again tonight, glaring at the men who passed by. He seemed meaner every time I saw him. I'd thought him quite timid at first, though I couldn't exactly call someone shy who walked around naked, could I?

A young Latino, with a chunky face and boobs slightly too prominent for someone only fifteen pounds overweight, walked by pretending to brush his hair behind his ears but really trying to flash his green wrist band.

Eric was here tonight. Jelani and Pranav, too. I didn't see Andrew, though with close to fifty guys in the room, it was hard to be sure. I didn't see Jamie, either. David, the Mark Spitz lookalike, stood near the padded bench, taking turns kissing and fondling three other men.

"Glad you could make it," Clayton said, walking up beside me. "You, too, detective."

Demir nodded, and I introduced Clayton and Tommy.

"Welcome aboard!" Clayton reached forward as if to shake Tommy's hand but instead headed for his cock. He paused just a moment, since Tommy wasn't wearing a wrist band of any color, and asked, "May I?"

Tommy nodded, and Clayton stroked him for a few moments before winking and turning to Demir.

"So much of my identity is wrapped up in this club," Clayton said. "You guys need to find the killer." He paused. "Or killers. Maybe the two murders are completely unrelated. Maybe it's two different murderers who don't even know each other. I mean, we talked about the two victims not being related but maybe it's the murderers who aren't."

As Clayton spoke, Demir casually reached over and began stroking him without asking, since Clayton wore a green wrist band. Clayton didn't even seem to notice, so used to being touched. But Demir caught my eye. He was conducting the emergency-room-nurse-at-the-dinner-table test.

Clayton passed.

A moment after he moved on, Chris sauntered over. Damn, he was a good looking man. "I got extra credit in my PI class with a report about the club murders," he said, looking at me while tweaking one of Tommy's nipples and cupping Demir, without asking any of us. No one seemed to mind, but then, given their blank expressions, it wasn't easy knowing what either Tommy or Demir was thinking.

"I had an A- going into the final, but I think this will get me to that full A." He shrugged with a smile. "Grades won't be out until the first of January."

The lights flickered, and I instinctively looked upward. When they came back on, Chris was licking Demir's nipples. Demir looked at me and raised an eyebrow. Another fellow walking by leaned in and kissed the detective on the mouth.

Tommy reached over and took my hand. "Thank you," he whispered.

Technically, he was still speaking loudly, given the music, just at a lower volume than he'd have needed for normal conversation. "Thank you for reawakening me."

"You are going to spore like a mushroom," I whispered back.

I'd been half-heartedly keeping an eye out for Sorrel, and just at that moment, I saw him near the sofa, setting a cup down on the end table. When he looked about nervously, I motioned to Demir and Tommy, and we all moved over toward him. I pointed to the video screen, so my buddies looked up while I casually reached for the cup.

Up on the huge screen, a black man ejaculated, a thick stream almost two feet long shooting out the end of his dick. It didn't seem physically possible. The shot was followed by that of another man, this one Latino, aiming his dick at the camera from at least two or three feet away. We could see the white glob heading our way, and then the lens was covered.

"Fuck," Tommy whispered.

I resisted the temptation to confirm what I hoped was in the water, slowly raising it to my lips but pausing as I continued to watch the video in fascination. A white man, reclining against his headboard, ejaculated with his mouth open. A huge stream landed directly across his face, splitting it into two equal halves, the only part of the dividing line missing that which had fallen across his tongue, where it had been quickly swallowed with a smile.

I tried to watch Sorrel out of the corner of my eye, but as soon as I paid attention to my peripheral vision, it seemed to become harder to see. I downed the water in the cup and saw Sorrel's dick twitch. Of course, there was so much stimulation in so many directions, his reaction might have had nothing to do with the cup.

I honestly couldn't tell if there was anything beyond water in there, diluted enough not to be remarkable, especially with the scent of semen already in the air. Still, I turned halfway in Sorrel's direction. "Mmm," I said, "they must be serving bottled water." Now I sniffed the cup deliberately, and this time, Sorrel's twitch was clearly correlated. "I wonder what brand. It's good." I sniffed again. "A hint of cucumber." I looked at Sorrel. "Damn. Now I want a cucumber."

Sorrel grinned and walked away.

I hoped I'd shown him a good time. He'd sure given me one.

And I suddenly turned to Tommy and stared. In addition to our other sexual incompatibilities, Tommy liked "dirty talk," while I could never manage it. One could only say, "Oh yeah" or "You're so hot" or "You feel so good," just so many times. I could offer approving moans and grunts at regular intervals but not words.

But now I wondered if I could simply try creating various scenarios out loud while Tommy and I had sex. I could never give him good head, given the size of his dick, but I could describe one of the men from tonight and say things like, "I dreamed about watching him kneel in front of you, licking your dick around the edges until a drop of pre-cum oozed out the top, and then licking the pre-cum off. I dreamed he leaned back and kissed me to give me your pre-cum and then went back to your dick."

On and on. I could keep making stuff up until Tommy finished fucking me, but at least he could be *thinking* about oral sex, since that was what he preferred. And he'd get the "dirty talk," too.

Why had this never occurred to me before?

"You okay?" Tommy asked.

"Thank you for reawakening *me*," I said.

I watched Tommy fondle a couple of guys, watched Demir play with several men, and was approached by one young Asian who asked if he could call me Daddy. "I'd rather we see each other as equals," I said. He walked off to find someone else. Oh, well. I couldn't accommodate everyone's fetishes.

I saw the young man talking to Howard, about fifteen years his senior. Howard nodded and then suddenly turned the twenty-year-old around before pulling him tightly against his chest. Howard's left arm held the younger man in a chokehold as he reached around and began roughly jacking the guy off with his right hand.

I caught Demir's eye and nodded toward the two men.

I felt a hand on my ass and turned around. "Hey, Bruce." Stu squeezed one of my cheeks.

Time to try gathering a bit more information. With the music so loud, it was difficult to guide the conversation, but as I stroked Stu, I finally managed. "What self-defense class are you signed up for? I need to train, too."

Stu frowned, and I realized I wasn't supposed to know about the class.

"I don't know what you're talking about," he said. He turned around and walked off.

Probably ten men had left the event by this point, but another few had joined shortly before Last Entry, so there were still plenty of dicks to go around. Tommy, Demir, and I moved over to the chaise longue for a while, then drifted toward the padded cube, and finally back to the massage table, where Demir lay face down. I'd never been brave enough.

Demir hadn't wanted to touch either of us too much, given the investigation, but he couldn't see who was touching him now. I was surprised to see several prominent freckles on his ass, seeming to form something approximating the Big Dipper. Tommy caressed Demir's ass, I caressed the back of his head, another man knelt to sniff his feet, and a fourth man beat off onto Demir's back.

I needed a pair of secret agent glasses with a hidden camera. Ah, the memory book I could make!

Tommy and I stood on opposite sides of the massage table, looked at one another, and beat off together, adding our spooge to that already pooling on Demir's back. Then Tommy grabbed a paper towel from one of the tables and wiped him off.

Demir climbed off the table, his dick hard as a board, and beat himself off, shooting onto the floor.

All of this was a lot more fun with Tommy by my side.

While these events often felt exotic, even a bit extreme, they simultaneously felt completely normal, or at least what I wanted normal to feel like. This was the way life should be lived.

I motioned toward the bathroom, and we headed off as a group. Thank God nothing awful had happened tonight. I'd accept never knowing who the killer was if it meant never hearing from him again.

We passed Clayton, who was fondling someone near the chaise longue. He beckoned me over and whispered in my ear. I could barely hear him this close to the speakers. "Chris found a dead rat in the kitchen earlier. I hope we finish tonight before a live one runs out."

What a totally weird thing to share.

"If you hear a high-pitched scream," I said, "I swear it's not me!"

I led the way into the hallway, Demir and Tommy right behind me. Chris came out of the bathroom, and his eyes lit up when he saw us. "Guys!" he said, pulling us into a huddle. "I think I know who the murderer is!"

"Who?" Demir demanded.

"It's Marin!" Chris glanced around quickly. "Look what I found in the kitchen when I was filling the water bottles."

He led us through the swinging doors to our right.

Demir didn't see the pipe before it struck him in the head. He dropped to the floor along with the pipe just as Chris grabbed a knife and held it to Tommy's throat.

"I'm really sorry, Bruce," he said. "But I know you already figured it out. You didn't leave me any choice."

Chapter Twenty

"Chris…"

Oh my god. But…but why? It didn't make sense.

"Please," I said, "let him go."

Chris gave me the look a teacher might give a slow child.

"Sal I get," I said. Everyone disliked Sal. "But why Peter?" In movies, the detectives always tried to keep the murderer talking, and help always arrived just in the nick of time. But Demir was the help, and he was unconscious, at least concussed and possibly already dead. I didn't even have time to check if he was breathing.

No one else ever came into the kitchen other than the volunteer filling water jugs before the event began. Our bodies might not be found until sometime Wednesday morning.

Or Thursday, since tomorrow was Christmas.

Porca la Madonna.

If only Tommy could get away. I couldn't remember if we'd gone over ways to get out of a headlock, but even if we had, those headlocks wouldn't have been accompanied by sharp knives at our throats. He'd either remember a trick or not.

I simply couldn't yell while that knife was pressed against Tommy's throat. And who would hear? We were already down the hall from the main room. Music was playing loudly out there. Porn, too. People were occupied. Preoccupied. And there was a guy out there shouting as he reached climax. Him I could hear over the loudspeakers.

How fast were those security guards? And how good were they? If they were straight, they were probably repulsed and just trying to get through the evening. If they were gay, they might be distracted. Were they out there, standing in a roomful of naked men, zoned out?

Why didn't Chris kill Tommy now? Every second he waited, there was a chance someone might stop him.

And I suddenly knew the answer. We'd come as a team tonight. If Tommy went down, I'd have a chance to run out and tell everyone what happened. Chris wouldn't get away this time. And he knew it.

Chris *couldn't* slit Tommy's throat. Not yet.

I slowly crouched down and picked up the metal pipe.

"Drop it!" Chris ordered.

"What did you have against Sal?" I asked. "Other than his being an asshole?"

Chris glared at me, glared at the pipe, and huffed. "He filmed us having sex without telling me," he said. "Made it look like I hadn't douched. And then posted the video online."

Sal really had been a creep. But was that a motive?

Why hadn't the police found the video? I'd never heard Demir say much about Chris being a possible suspect.

But then, how many sex videos out there would be tagged with the names of the participants?

"Couldn't you just humiliate him back?" I asked.

Chris pressed the knife deeper against Tommy's throat. I could see a thin, red line on his light brown skin. I tightened my grip on the pipe.

"Oh, there's plenty more to it than that."

"And Peter?" I asked, moving just an inch closer.

He snorted. "We used to work at the same company. Not in the same department, but we knew of each other. I had another coworker I hated. And I killed that guy outside his house one night."

My gasp this time wasn't particularly gay. "You—you what?"

"I've always been fascinated by crime," Chris went on. "I'd taken a couple of piddly courses online before." He scoffed again. "You'd be surprised how easy it is to get away with murder." He smiled. "That's why I killed that bastard from work."

The knife was slightly away from Tommy's skin, but not far enough. I moved another quarter of an inch toward them.

"I studied hard this semester so I could learn how to better cover my tracks." He paused. "Every time."

I felt a chill run through me, which forced a drop of urine to the tip of my penis.

"Practice makes perfect."

"But why Peter? Did he know about the coworker?"

Chris smiled. "He did after our talk tonight."

We were all standing in the crowded kitchen stark naked. Clean pots and pans were stacked in the sink behind us, a trolley filled with metal trays blocked the other sink from view. Out of the corner of my eye, I saw Tommy lowering one arm. I couldn't divert my focus without giving him away, but I hoped he was about to reach back and grab Chris's balls. I'd be ready when he did.

"See that?" Chris motioned with his head.

I followed his gaze and saw a hypodermic on the edge of a counter.

"You're going to inject yourself."

"And why would I do that?"

"Because I'll kill your husband if you don't."

"You'll kill him anyway," I said. "If I run out of here, his murderer will at least face justice. That's the least I can do for the man I love."

Chris paused, unsure if I was being serious or not.

"You'll inject yourself or I'll emasculate him," Chris said. "Then I'll cut off your detective's dick."

Detective Downey clearly wasn't on her way here to rescue us. Why hadn't Clayton ordered the security guards to make rounds? Tonight's event wouldn't be over for another thirty or forty minutes. I had to figure something out immediately. I held out my hand. "Take me and let him go."

"Drop the pipe."

I took a deep breath and belted out at the top of my lungs, "Ye elders of Israel, come join now with me!"

Chris looked stunned. Tommy reached back and squeezed. And Demir swept his legs out and knocked Chris off his feet. I screamed at the top of my lungs.

Somehow, the combination of attacks paralyzed the man just long enough for Tommy to wrench himself away. I swung the pipe against Chris's arm and heard a loud *crack* as he dropped the knife. Tommy helped Demir to his feet, and together they piled on top of the biggest creep I'd ever known. The security guards rushed in a moment later.

Epilogue. Five Months Later.

For someone who wanted to hide his crimes, Chris ended up talking quite openly once it was clear he was going down at least for the assault on Demir and Tommy's attempted murder. He claimed to have killed two other people even before murdering his coworker years ago, and one other person in between that killing and Sal's.

None of the other murders were of gay men. He'd only recently turned his hatred toward his own kind.

Chris's arrest and the revelation of the additional murders barely stayed in the news twenty-four hours. There was way too much else going on in the world.

Our fears about the new regime had been justified. By the start of the administration's fifth month, over 40% of Project 2025 had already been implemented. Green card holders and even naturalized citizens who'd committed no crimes were kidnapped by masked men in broad daylight and whisked off to private prisons in other countries. The genocide in Gaza continued to escalate. The war in Ukraine as well, which didn't stop the administration from rescinding the refugee status of 280,000 Ukrainian immigrants.

Judges and elected officials just doing their jobs were arrested, their only crime disagreeing with fascist policies.

Media was targeted, and universities, even law firms. Transgender troops were expelled from the military. Hundreds of thousands of federal employees were fired or forced to resign. Tariffs of 25%, 50%, even 145% were added onto goods from virtually every country.

The despot-in-chief threatened to annex Canada and make it our 51st state.

Tommy and I told our friends in Canada not to visit.

Books about LGBTQ history, black history, Native American history, and more were removed from public school libraries. And from U.S. military libraries and websites. Funding for PBS, NPR, Medicaid, FEMA, NIH, CDC, and many more programs and departments were slashed. Huge tax cuts for the rich were paid by gutting SNAP benefits and school lunch programs. Social Security and Medicare were in the crosshairs.

MAGA politicians just shrugged and said, "Well, everybody dies sometime."

Small D democratic Americans fought back, protesting weekly in towns large and small across the country. They boycotted fascist brands. They called their senators and representatives again and again. They filed lawsuits. And they protested even more.

Tommy and I tried to live our lives as best we could. I requested vacation leave in advance for the days I knew major protests were planned so I could participate. I was arrested—and then released without charge—while counter protesting an anti-trans hate rally on Capitol Hill. Tommy never missed a single Saturday protesting outside a fascist car dealership in Renton.

Nathan and I continued protesting genocide. Going to the occasional movie. Having dinner in Columbia City.

And I continued sucking his dick.

The regime would fall sooner or later. Regimes always did…eventually. But life was never going to be the same even in a best-case scenario.

Meanwhile, Tommy, Demir, and I became better friends. Tommy and I played more Scrabble, adding Boggle and Upwords to our game options. And soon the three of us were playing Scrabble together. Demir was better at it than I was, too, even before throwing in the occasional Turkish word.

Tommy and I now had sex at least once a week. Tommy and Demir began a sexual friendship, too. Demir's mouth, it turned out, could accommodate Tommy's huge cock. Demir and I began a sexual relationship as well.

The man was decidedly odd. We got along great.

Tommy came up with the idea of purchasing a raffle drum, that device folks used to spin raffle tickets. We all wrote a variety of sexual activities we enjoyed or would like to try, and every couple of weeks, we'd spin the drum and explore the possibilities.

We had a separate raffle drum for date ideas.

Tommy and I watched a remake of *The Wedding Banquet*. Demir and I watched more Turkish television. And we all watched reruns of *Dark Winds*, since Demir enjoyed critiquing detective series in a way to help us understand his work. The three of us formed our own little book club, where we'd choose a detective novel and then analyze it every few chapters to see how we were processing the clues.

And we all continued playing at Jack Off Buddies a couple of times a month.

It wasn't clear we'd ever become a throuple, but we were increasingly exploring the possibility. For now, we spent the entire night together just once a week, usually at our home in south Seattle.

Demir led us in self-defense classes at his home on Beacon Hill. They frequently ended with a shower, a massage, and happy endings. Positive reinforcement, he called it.

Tommy was also taking PI classes, "just for fun."

This afternoon at work, I received a text.

Tommy: 92 degrees on Sat. Another record.

Me: Ugh.

Demir: Sweaty.

We had established a routine group chat.

Tommy: Let's go to Rialto Beach.

Demir: I'll take the day off.

Me: I'll buy some healthy snacks.

The fight against oppression was never over. Or the everyday fight against crime. Neither was the fight to maintain and strengthen relationships. "Put Your Shoulder to the Wheel" and all that. So we kept plugging on as if our lives depended on it.

Because the alternative, one way or another, was death.

Books by Johnny Townsend

Thanks for reading! If you enjoyed this book, could you please take a few minutes to write a review online? Reviews are helpful both to me as an author and to other readers, so we'd all sincerely appreciate your writing one! And if you did enjoy the book, here are some others I've written you might want to look up:

Mormon Underwear

A Gay Mormon Missionary in Pompeii

The Golem of Rabbi Loew

Marginal Mormons

Sexual Solidarity

The Mysterious Madness of Mormons

Going-Out-Of-Religion Sale

Escape from Zion

Gayrabian Nights

Invasion of the Spirit Snatchers

Sins of the Saints

Mormon Misfits

Gay Gaslighting

Out of the Missionary's Closet

A Mormon Motive for Murder

Breaking the Promise of the Promised Land

Mormon Misfits

I Will, Through the Veil

Am I My Planet's Keeper?

Have Your Cum and Eat It, Too

Strangers with Benefits

Constructing Equity

Wake Up and Smell the Missionaries

Racism by Proxy

Orgy at the STD Clinic

Please Evacuate

Recommended Daily Humanity

The Camper Killings

Repent! The End of Capitalism is Nigh!

Brace for Impact

10 Things to Do Before the Apocalypse

Murder at the Jack Off Club

Kinky Quilts: Patchwork Designs for Gay Men

An Eternity of Mirrors: Best Short Stories of Johnny Townsend

Inferno in the French Quarter: The UpStairs Lounge Fire

Latter-Gay Saints: An Anthology of Gay Mormon Fiction (co-editor)

Available from your favorite online or neighborhood bookstore.

Wondering what some of those other books are about? Read on!

Gayrabian Nights

Gayrabian Nights is a twist on the well-known classic, *1001 Arabian Nights*, in which Scheherazade, under the threat of death if she ceases to captivate King Shahryar's attention, enchants him through a series of mysterious, adventurous, and romantic tales.

In this variation, a male escort, invited to the hotel room of a closeted, homophobic Mormon senator, learns that the man is poised to vote on a piece of anti-gay legislation the following morning. To prevent him from sleeping, so that the exhausted senator will miss casting his vote on the Senate floor, the escort entertains him with stories of homophobia, celibacy, mixed orientation marriages, reparative therapy, coming out, first love, gay marriage, and long-term successful gay relationships.

The escort crafts the stories to give the senator a crash course in gay culture and sensibilities, hoping to bring the man closer to accepting his own sexual orientation.

Inferno in the French Quarter: The UpStairs Lounge Fire

On Gay Pride Day in 1973, someone set the entrance to a French Quarter gay bar on fire. In the terrible inferno that followed, thirty-two people lost their lives, including a third of the local congregation of the Metropolitan Community Church, their pastor burning to death halfway out a second-story window as he tried to claw his way to freedom.

A mother who'd gone to the bar with her two gay sons died alongside them. A man who'd helped his friend escape first was found dead near the fire escape. Two children waited outside a movie theater across town for a father and "uncle" who would never pick them up. During this era of rampant homophobia, several families refused to claim the bodies, and many churches refused to bury the dead.

Author Johnny Townsend pored through old records and tracked down survivors of the fire as well as relatives and friends of those killed to compile this fascinating account of a forgotten moment in gay history.

This second edition on the 50th anniversary of the fire includes additional research and information not available previously.

The Golem of Rabbi Loew

Jacob and Esau Cohen are the closest of brothers. In fact, they're lovers. A doctor tries to combine canine genes with those of Jews, to improve their chances of surviving a hostile world. A Talmudic scholar dates an escort. A scientist tries to develop the

"God spot" in the brains of his patients in hopes of creating a messiah.

A Jew-by-Choice navigates Jewish/Muslim relations during Pesach. A gay Lubavitcher dating a Catholic is attacked and left for dead but becomes a police officer in response. The Golem of Prague is really Rabbi Loew's secret lover.

While some of the Jews in Townsend's book are Orthodox, this collection of Jewish stories most certainly is not.

Orgy at the STD Clinic

Todd Tillotson is struggling to move on after his husband is killed in a hit and run attack a year earlier during a Black Lives Matter protest in Seattle.

In this novel set entirely on public transportation, we watch as Todd, isolated throughout the pandemic, battles desperation in his attempt to safely reconnect with the world.

Will he find love again, even casual friendship, or will he simply end up another crazy old man on the bus?

Things don't look good until a man whose face he can't even see sits down beside him despite the raging variants.

And asks him a question that will change his life.

Please Evacuate

A gay, partygoing New Yorker unconcerned about the future or the unsustainability of capitalism is hit by a truck and thrust into a straight man's body half a continent away. As Hunter tries to figure out what's happening, he's caught up in another disaster, a wildfire sweeping through a Colorado community, the flames overtaking him and several schoolchildren as they flee.

When he awakens, Hunter finds himself in the body of yet another man, this time in northern Italy, a former missionary about to marry a young Mormon woman. Still piecing together this new reality, and beginning to embrace his latest identity, Hunter fights for his life in a devastating flash flood along with his wife *and* his new husband.

He's an aging worker in drought-stricken Texas, a nurse at an assisted living facility in the direct path of a hurricane, an advocate for the unhoused during a freak Seattle blizzard.

We watch as Hunter is plunged into life after life, finally recognizing the futility of only looking out for #1 and understanding the part he must play in addressing the global climate crisis…if he ever gets another chance.

Kinky Quilts

Since patchwork quilts are usually displayed in bedrooms where couples engage in sex, why are there so few quilt designs for folks who want a bit of sexual energy in these intimate spaces?

The original designs in this volume range from simple to intermediate, and with over 250 to choose from, even beginner quilters will find patterns tempting enough to get started.

In *Kinky Quilts*, Johnny Townsend has collected his best designs from *Quilting Beyond the Rainbow*, *Gay Sleeping Arrangements*, and *Queer Quilting*, to offer fun, sexy quilts for men who love men.

10 Things to Do Before the Apocalypse

When happily married Jake and Santino head to the bars on Seattle's Capitol Hill to pick up a third for the night, they don't realize they're about to hook up with a dead man.

Only they can see and interact with Andy, stabbed to death near Pioneer Square a few days earlier. Finally convinced that Andy really has been murdered, Jake and Santino join forces with his ghost to track down the killer.

Did Andy's jealous ex do it? His spurned coworker? A right-wing vigilante?

As the trio investigates, police and coworkers begin to suspect Jake and Santino may be mentally ill...or the murderers themselves.

Will they be arrested? Institutionalized?

Amidst escalating political tensions, Jake and Santino begin to fall in love with Andy. But what will become of him when the killer is found?

And what happens if the killer comes after Jake and Santino next?

Brace for Impact

As Craig and Toby struggle to keep their faltering marriage alive, the climate crisis intrudes, part of a threesome in their relationship. Craig wants to take drastic action but Toby just wants to live his life as best he can before climate breakdown escalates.

"You fight for your life by any means necessary," Craig insists. "If someone breaks into your house, you pull out a baseball bag or a gun. When there's a mass shooting, you run, hide, or fight back."

But when it involves global warming? And fossil fuel industries buying politicians who protect carbon emissions at the cost of human lives? Craig wonders if a letter to the editor is effective. If blocking traffic at a rally once or twice a year is enough.

Toby threatens to leave him if he does anything stupid. And to report him to the authorities.

But Craig feels he'll need to commit violence one way or another, either by condoning the status quo or by doing whatever he can to fight those who keep destabilizing the climate. So he joins a group of eco activists whose efforts are far more extreme than even he had expected.

Will Craig survive the violent police crackdown on protesters? Will his relationship with Toby survive the additional stress of betrayal?

And will either of them survive the new wildfire that's just started at the edge of town?

Have Your Cum and Eat It, Too

It's 1981, and two Mormon missionaries randomly assigned to work together as "companions" in Napoli find themselves in trouble. They're falling in love, but the Church forbids gay relationships. As missionaries, they can't date anyone at all, much less other men. If they're found out, they'll be excommunicated, sent home in disgrace, and cast out from their families.

In the aftermath of a devastating earthquake, against a backdrop of poverty and repressive mission culture, Elders Grant and Mortensen knock on doors, endure violent assaults, and face the ultimate challenge—will they be crushed by dedication to their beliefs or will love provide a way for them to escape?

An Eternity of Mirrors

From over 500 short stories published over three decades, author Johnny Townsend presents several of his favorites.

A gay couple steals from the rich to support their favorite charities.

Two young women vie for the affections of the same missionary.

A father with a speech impediment is forced into the spotlight after his daughter survives a school shooting.

A reporter seeks the identity of Salt Lake's new superhero—a masked man wearing temple clothes who mysteriously shows up at crime scenes.

Two young missionaries in the Pacific Northwest sneak out on a date.

An uncle awaits word on his niece caught up in the 2004 tsunami.

Missionaries in Rome try to prevent a terrorist bombing.

Townsend's favorite stories celebrate life and love in a troubled world.

What Readers Have Said

Townsend's stories are "a gay *Portnoy's Complaint* of Mormonism. Salacious, sweet, sad, insightful, insulting, religiously ethnic, quirky-faithful, and funny."

D. Michael Quinn, author of *The Mormon Hierarchy: Origins of Power*

"Told from a believably conversational first-person perspective, [*A Gay Mormon Missionary in Pompeii*'s] novelistic focus on Anderson's journey to thoughtful self-acceptance allows for greater character development than often seen in short stories, which makes this well-paced work rich and satisfying, and one of Townsend's strongest. An extremely important contribution to the field of Mormon fiction." Named to Kirkus Reviews' Best of 2011.

Kirkus Reviews

"The thirteen stories in *Mormon Underwear* capture this struggle [between Mormonism and homosexuality] with humor, sadness, insight, and sometimes shocking details....*Mormon Underwear* provides compelling stories, literally from the inside-out."

Niki D'Andrea, *Phoenix New Times*

"Townsend's lively writing style and engaging characters [in *Zombies for Jesus*] make for stories which force us to wake up, smell the (prohibited) coffee, and review our attitudes with regard to reading dogma so doggedly. These are tales which revel in the individual tics and quirks which make us human, Mormon or not, gay or not…"

A.J. Kirby, *The Short Review*

"The Rift," from *A Gay Mormon Missionary in Pompeii*, is a "fascinating tale of an untenable situation…a *tour de force*."

David Lenson, editor, *The Massachusetts Review*

"Pronouncing the Apostrophe," from *The Golem of Rabbi Loew*, is "quiet and revealing, an intriguing tale…"

Sima Rabinowitz, Literary Magazine Review, *NewPages.com*

The Circumcision of God is "a collection of short stories that consider the imperfect, silenced majority of Mormons, who may in fact be [the Church's] best hope.…[The book leaves] readers regretting the church's willingness to marginalize those who best exemplify its ideals: those who love fiercely despite all obstacles, who brave challenges at great personal risk and who always choose the hard, higher road."

Kirkus Reviews

In *Mormon Fairy Tales*, Johnny Townsend displays "both a wicked sense of irony and a deep well of compassion."

Kel Munger, *Sacramento News and Review*

Zombies for Jesus is "eerie, erotic, and magical."

Publishers Weekly

"While [Townsend's] many touching vignettes draw deeply from Mormon mythology, history, spirituality and culture, [*Mormon Fairy Tales*] is neither a gaudy act of proselytism nor angry protest literature from an ex-believer. Like all good fiction, his stories are simply about the joys, the hopes and the sorrows of people."

Kirkus Reviews

"In *Inferno in the French Quarter* author Johnny Townsend restores this tragic event [the UpStairs Lounge fire] to its proper place in LGBT history and reminds us that the victims of the blaze were not just 'statistics,' but real people with real lives, families, and friends."

Jesse Monteagudo, *The Bilerico Project*

In *Inferno in the French Quarter*, "Townsend's heart-rending descriptions of the victims…seem to [make them] come alive once more."

Kit Van Cleave, *OutSmart Magazine*

"While [*Inferno in the French Quarter*] is a non-fiction work, the author is a skilled fiction [writer], so he manages to respect the realism of the story, while at the same time recreating their lives and voices. It's probably thanks to the [author's] skills that this piece of non-fiction goes well beyond a simple recording of events."

Elisa Rolle, *Rainbow Awards*

Marginal Mormons is "an irreverent, honest look at life outside the mainstream Mormon Church….Throughout his musings on sin and forgiveness, Townsend beautifully demonstrates his characters' internal, perhaps irreconcilable struggles….Rather than anger and disdain, he offers an honest portrayal of people searching for meaning and community in their lives, regardless of their life choices or secrets." Named to Kirkus Reviews' Best of 2012.

Kirkus Reviews

The stories in *The Mormon Victorian Society* "register the new openness and confidence of gay life in the age of same-sex marriage….What hasn't changed is Townsend's wry, conversational prose, his subtle evocations of character and social dynamics, and his deadpan humor. His warm empathy still glows in this intimate yet clear-eyed engagement with Mormon theology and folkways. Funny, shrewd and finely wrought dissections of the awkward contradictions—and surprising harmonies—between conscience and desire." Named to Kirkus Reviews' Best of 2013.

Kirkus Reviews

"This collection of short stories [*The Mormon Victorian Society*] featuring gay Mormon characters slammed [me] in the face from the first page, wrestled my heart and mind to the floor, and left me panting and wanting more by the end. Johnny Townsend has created so many memorable characters in such few pages. I went weeks thinking about this book. It truly touched me."

Tom Webb, *A Bear on Books*

Dragons of the Book of Mormon is an "entertaining collection....Townsend's prose is sharp, clear, and easy to read, and his characters are well rendered..."

Publishers Weekly

"The pre-eminent documenter of alternative Mormon lifestyles...Townsend has a deep understanding of his characters, and his limpid prose, dry humor and well-grounded (occasionally magical) realism make their spiritual conundrums both compelling and entertaining. [*Dragons of the Book of Mormon* is] [a]nother of Townsend's critical but affectionate and absorbing tours of Mormon discontent." Named to Kirkus Reviews' Best of 2014.

Kirkus Reviews

In *Gayrabian Nights*, "Townsend's prose is always limpid and evocative, and…he finds real drama and emotional depth in the most ordinary of lives."

Kirkus Reviews

Gayrabian Nights is a "complex revelation of how seriously soul damaging the denial of the true self can be."

Ryan Rhodes, author of *Free Electricity*

Gayrabian Nights "was easily the most original book I've read all year. Funny, touching, topical, and thoroughly enjoyable."

Rainbow Awards

Lying for the Lord is "one of the most gripping books that I've picked up for quite a while. I love the author's writing style, alternately cynical, humorous, biting, scathing, poignant, and touching…. This is the third book of his that I've read, and all are equally engaging. These are stories that need to be told, and the author does it in just the right way."

Heidi Alsop, *Ex-Mormon Foundation Board Member*

In *Lying for the Lord*, Townsend "gets under the skin of his characters to reveal their complexity and conflicts....shrewd, evocative [and] wryly humorous."

Kirkus Reviews

In *Missionaries Make the Best Companions*, "the author treats the clash between religious dogma and liberal humanism with vivid realism, sly humor, and subtle feeling as his characters try to figure out their true missions in life. Another of Townsend's rich dissections of Mormon failures and uncertainties…" Named to Kirkus Reviews' Best of 2015.

Kirkus Reviews

In *Invasion of the Spirit Snatchers*, "Townsend, a confident and practiced storyteller, skewers the hypocrisies and eccentricities of his characters with precision and affection. The outlandish framing narrative is the most consistent source of shock and humor, but the stories do much to ground the reader in the world—or former world—of the characters....A funny, charming tale about a group of Mormons facing the end of the world."

Kirkus Reviews

"Townsend's collection [*The Washing of Brains*] once again displays his limpid, naturalistic prose, skillful narrative chops, and his subtle insights into psychology…Well-crafted dispatches on the clash between religion and self-fulfillment…"

Kirkus Reviews

"While the author is generally at his best when working as a satirist, there are some fine, understated touches in these tales [*The Last Days Linger*] that will likely affect readers in subtle ways….readers should come away impressed by the deep empathy he shows for all his characters—even the homophobic ones."

Kirkus Reviews

"Written in a conversational style that often uses stories and personal anecdotes to reveal larger truths, this immensely approachable book [*Racism by Proxy*] skillfully serves its intended audience of White readers grappling with complex questions regarding race, history, and identity. The author's frequent references to the Church of Jesus Christ of Latter-day Saints may be too niche for readers unfamiliar with its idiosyncrasies, but Townsend generally strikes a perfect balance of humor, introspection, and reasoned arguments that will engage even skeptical readers."

Kirkus Reviews

Selling the City of Enoch is "sharply intelligent…pleasingly complex…The stories are full of…doubters, but there's no vindictiveness in these pages; the characters continuously poke holes in Mormonism's more extravagant absurdities, but they take very little pleasure in doing so….Many of Townsend's stories…have a provocative edge to them, but this [book] displays a great deal of insight as well…a playful, biting and surprisingly warm collection."

Kirkus Reviews

Orgy at the STD Clinic portrays "an all-too real scenario that Townsend skewers to wincingly accurate proportions…[with] instant classic moments courtesy of his punchy, sassy, sexy lead character…"

Jim Piechota, *Bay Area Reporter*

Orgy at the STD Clinic is "…a triumph of humane sensibility. A richly textured saga that brilliantly captures the fraying social fabric of contemporary life." Named to Kirkus Reviews' Best Indie Books of 2022.

Kirkus Reviews

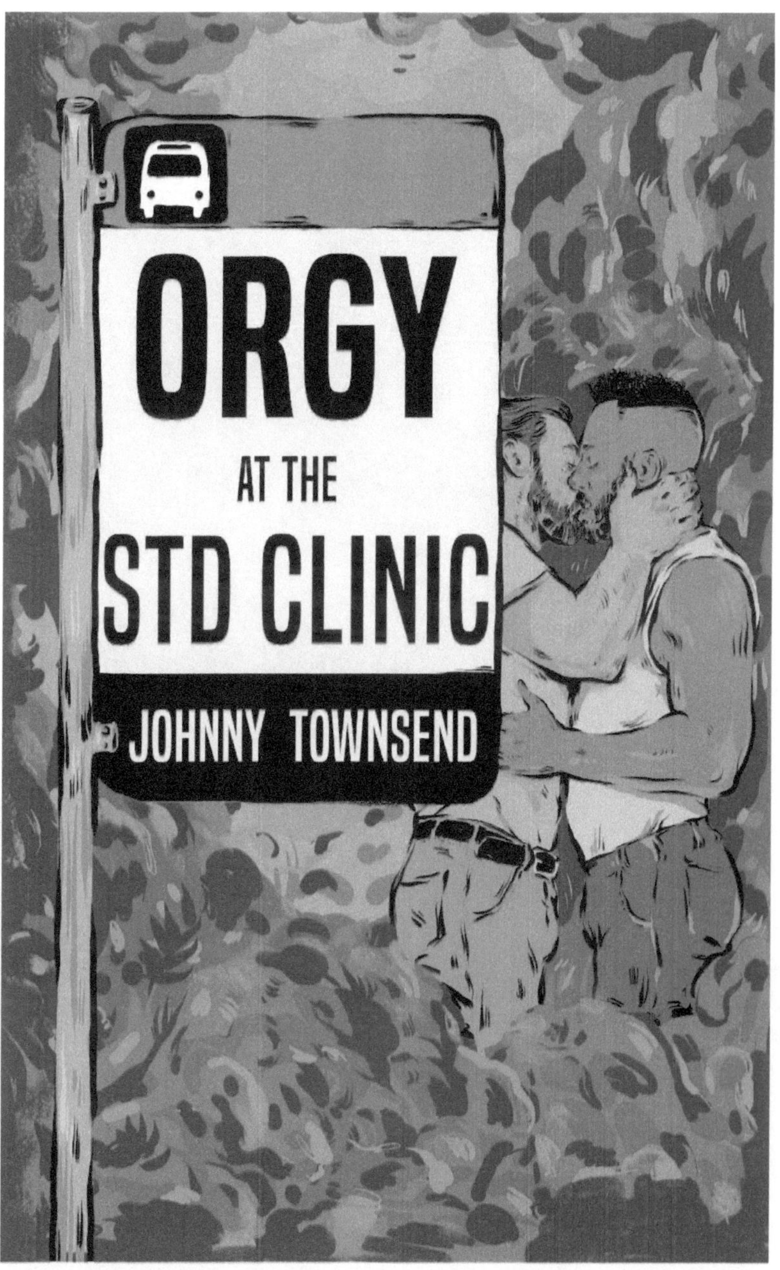
ORGY
AT THE
STD CLINIC
JOHNNY TOWNSEND

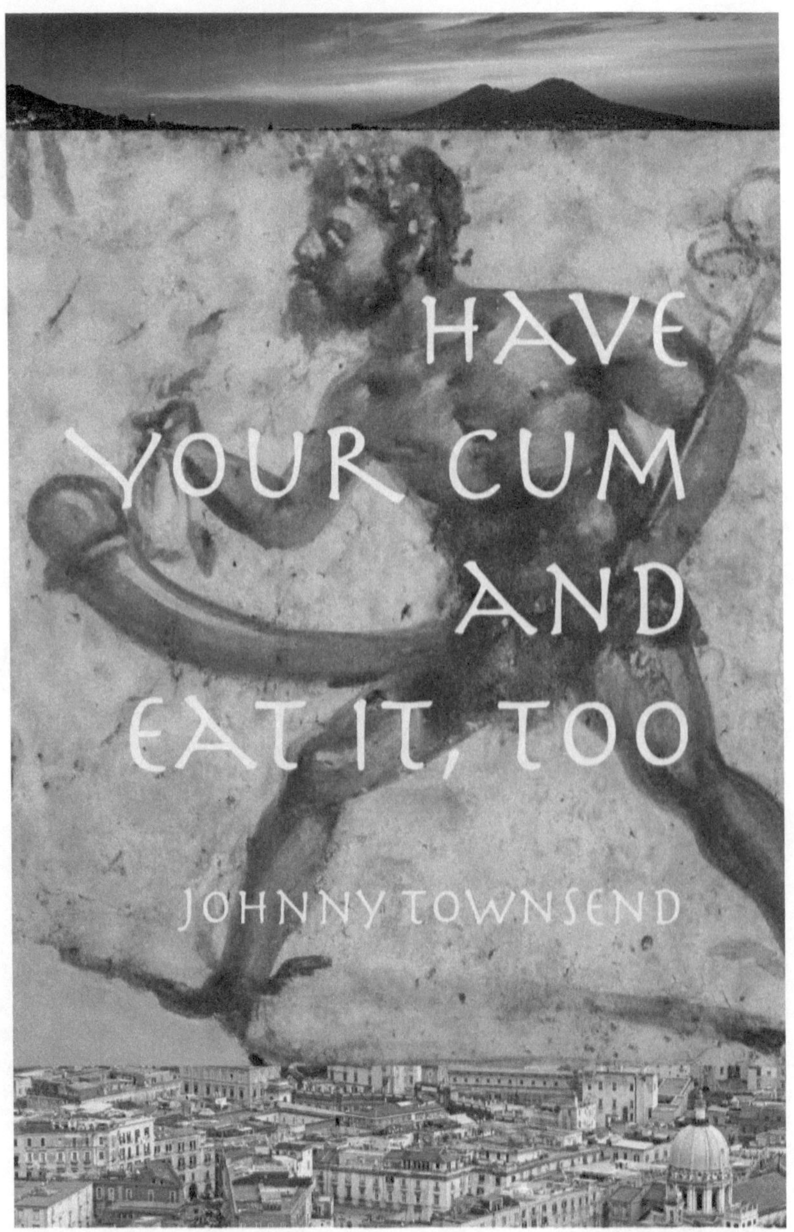
HAVE YOUR CUM AND EAT IT, TOO
JOHNNY TOWNSEND